I0831891

Did we really write this?

A JOC Anthology

First published by Making Magic Happen Academy 2017

Cover design by Karen Mc Dermott

This is a work of fiction. Names, characters, businesses, places, events and incidents are either the products of the author'/s' imagination or used in a fictitious manner. Any resemblance to actual persons, living or dead, or actual events is purely coincidental.

Because of the dynamic nature of the Internet, any web addresses or links contained in this book may have changed since publication and may no longer be valid. The views expressed in this work are solely those of the authors and do not necessarily reflect the views of the publisher and the publisher hereby disclaims any responsibility for them.

National Library of Australia

Cataloguing-in-Publication data:

ISBN: 978-0-6481030-8-0 (hc)

ISBN: 978-0-6481030-9-7 (e)

- Fiction

Making Magic Happen Academy books may be ordered through online booksellers or by contacting:

www.makingmagichappenacademy.com

ACKNOWLEDGEMENT

We want to thank JOC Wellness & Recovery for giving us the time and support to realise our combined dream of being published authors. Each member of this group would not have gotten here without the faith and patience of JOC. Through their belief we have grown not just as authors but as individuals. One book down and how many more to follow?

DEDICATION

Matt, this book is dedicated to you. Thank you for your loyalty and commitment. We know there is still room for growth and we promise to knock the doorways out when your head does. Without you and your faith in us I don't believe any one of us would have attempted this venture.

CONTENTS

DUST

Raymond L. Henderson

A billion years ago two suns were locked in a titanic battle; the efforts of a red and blue giant, each trying to absorb the other, yet so equal were their masses that neither could. Due to the immense gravitational pull of the colliding stars a smaller, yellow dwarf was drawn into the struggle. Although large compared to our own sun, its size was dwarfed by the other two. Slowly the dwarf was drawn between the two warring giants, pulled by the gravitation of the greater stars until the dwarf began to be torn down to its core. There it stayed for millions of years being torn apart atom by atom, a slow and agonising torture. All the while new elements were produced, new atomic structures created within those swirling fiery depths.

As the years passed the struggle for gravitational supremacy continued until one day the red giant weakened. If they had been sentient beings the blue giant could not have seized upon the opportunity faster. As rapidly as a gargantuan star could move, the blue giant absorbed the red, transforming itself into a super-giant. The sudden shift in gravitational forces was enough to allow the small sun to slingshot back out into space. Once free from the gravitational forces which had broken down its structure yet kept it stable by sheer force, the dwarf star exploded into a fine gas which bled throughout the cosmos. After millennia of constantly shifting temperatures, the gas was condensed, frozen, thawed until slowly solidifying to become dust at the atomic level.

Interstellar winds blew the dust arbitrarily throughout the solar systems until it began to drift towards a small blue planet. A planet where man had not yet taken his first steps. Unbeknown to man this dust would have future devastating consequences on their ability to use electricity.

The dust finally reached Earth a week before Christmas 1998 but its effects could not be felt right away as the dust was settling thin in the air, the world at the moment in limbo as people enjoyed the approaching holiday. For John Cater the night was the usual busy Friday. In this town the end of the work week was the prelude to the weekend nightclub violence, theft and drunk and disorderly complaints. Tonight there was a string of break-ins as criminals tried to steal the ample holiday wares. It was all drug related and John knew the thieves would be out in force looking for anything they could fence for a little bit of their own Christmas cheer.

It was not long before he got a call and pulled out of the car park where he had been trying to get a bite to eat, but as always duty came first when you wore the badge. He flipped on the siren for no reason than it woke him from the drowsiness he was feeling. The night went quickly and by six a.m. he was back in the station changing into street clothes, as was his habit before he went home.

At home his wife Ann had risen and was preparing breakfast for the three of them; his nine- year-old daughter, Devina was preparing for school. He welcomed them with hugs all round. “How was work?” Ann asked, the flatness of tone part of her mechanical enquiry each time he worked late.

“Busy, I made two arrests after a car chase,” John replied, though wondered why because it wasn’t like she actually cared.

Ann shuddered, she hated car chases and the dangers that went with them. Police work was dangerous enough without the dangers of high speed chases.

Time went quickly as it always does when you are in the usual routine; taking Devina to school, spending time with his wife, mowing the lawn, picking his daughter up from school, eating dinner, then to sleep. The days turned into weeks with the same inexorable pace as John’s daily life. No one noticed as the dust built up in the atmosphere. Each day was just a carbon copy of the last.

It was well into the New Year when things started to change. The first issue to manifest that people noticed was with small batteries that went flat even while still in their packaging. It was more of an annoyance than an actual problem; batteries could easily be recharged anyway. As this didn’t happen worldwide but only in isolated pockets, no one took any real notice.

To Ann shopping was the greatest irritation of any day and she did as little of it as possible. “The crowds were terrible,” she complained to John.

“You always say that.” John told her.

“Well it was,” she protested, though also flashing John a coy smile, knowing how petulant she sounded.

John smiled at his wife. After fifteen years of marriage if he wasn’t used to it by now he never would be. The trouble with Ann though, was she didn’t worry about having much food in the house. After years responding to emergencies John insisted on having enough food to last them for four months, and this caused friction between him and Ann. As he was helping Ann to put the groceries away he thought about their life together and marvelled that someone like Ann could fall for a bloke like him. She was a lady while John was a rough outdoors type, more happy hunting and fishing. Still if it was live theatre that Ann was interested in, so was he, be it reluctantly. The kitchen cupboards were full, as were the shelves that lined the walls of their double garage. They had so much preserved food that John estimated that with a bit of rationing he could make it last six months.

Apart from his need for preparation fostered by years of police service, John was like this from his memories of childhood. His parents had gone through hard times where they had no food to feed their kids. From the day things got better they had always kept a supply of food just in case. John had picked up this habit, much to his wife’s annoyance. It was lucky that she was willing to put up with it and the camping that she knew John was into. From the time they had first met John had always been a survivalist.

Across town Abel Sim, a thirty-year-old truck driver was just arriving home and greeted his twenty-seven-year-old wife Rami. “Hello, wife,” he said formally.

“Hello, husband,” she returned as formally, as he bent to kiss her forehead, she being six inches shorter than his six foot frame.

He removed a beer from the fridge and moved to his favourite chair. Rami worked in the kitchen preparing her husband's meal. She knew not to disturb him until after he had eaten, then they would chat about their days and their future.

Abel and Rami were from India and had been in Australia for six years; both spoke excellent English. They had a wide collection of friends inside the Indian community and a smattering of friends outside of it. He was not a strict husband like some of the other men Rami had met. In fact he was inclined to be too much the other way and let her get away with too much, and as much as she liked the freedom she also liked him being the boss. It was complicated, the way she felt, and though she had talked to her best friend about it she still didn't understand why she felt the way she did.

Their food was fresh because Rami went to the market three times a week and very little was held in the home. Abel liked it that way as he wouldn't eat frozen or canned food. They didn't have any children in their marriage as Abel was infertile and they had both agreed children were not an issue even though secretly Rami would have loved kids. It was after the meal when the dishes had been washed and put away that they talked about their worries and their future and Abel told her about his day and she hers, and all was well in the little world they had built for themselves.

In Germany Karl Frits was having a bad day, he was late for an important meeting and his car wouldn't start. Making things worse, the battery in his phone was flat even though he had charged it overnight, meaning he couldn't even call a taxi. Angrily he threw the offending phone against the garage wall where it shattered, then stomped out of the doorway. There was only one thing to do, he realised, and that was to catch a bus and hope the meeting could still go on.

In England Brad Hollinger was suffering the same trouble, only this time it was personal. The batteries in his radio were flat so he couldn't listen to the races; as he was in a wheelchair it was his only pleasure. His mate Tony would come around in the morning and place all his bets for the day. Brad had been injured at work and the compensation payment gave him a small pension to live on. He lived in a council flat and had a woman come in twice a week to clean.

And so it went around the world with millions of stories. Energy was being lost again and again; still it wasn't wide spread and no one connected the incidents to each other, after all who really pays attention to their last flat battery? The world continued to orbit the sun oblivious to its fate.

John was getting frustrated with Devina's demands for new batteries for her toys, the computer was playing up and the car battery would go flat if left two days without running the car.

"Dad, the computer won't work properly," Devina complained.

"I don't know what's wrong with it, you'll just have to put up with it," he replied impatiently.

"But Dad," she began.

"No buts, Devina, just play your game," he growled.

Devina knew better than to push her dad when he was in that sort of mood so she kept quiet. Still, she wondered what was wrong with her computer.

That's exactly what David James was thinking as he struggled to keep the computers on line. The company was computer based and couldn't afford to be off line without losing millions of dollars, so David struggled on, falling further behind every hour that passed. There was nothing that seemed to go right and he was getting more frustrated as time went on.

In Washington Major Ken Worth reported to General Taget's office as ordered and once there the General handed him a file. "I have a meeting so read this and we will talk after." David was taken aback by the General's abruptness but nevertheless settled down to read the file.

Top Secret

The armed forces are having major trouble with their computers, leaving them at a disadvantage. At this time it is limited in scope yet it is becoming alarmingly apparent that if the trend continues we will lose our ability to defend ourselves and may have to think about recalling the troops from overseas to help with security at home.

According to the President's advisors, society could become disrupted with the loss of computers and as the world's economy is run by computers we can envisage widespread disturbance to daily life.

However it should only take a few weeks to solve the problem and restore everything to normal. The President's advisors have assured him there is nothing to worry about as the public will quickly adapt to the situation and help each other through the few weeks that will be needed.

The real cause of the computer problem could be centred on strange dust that has been found in the atmosphere, so fine as to be unseeable by the naked eye. However according to Dr Write of the Atmospheric Institute this would be impossible as the air all around us is full of dust and the only trouble it gives is if there's a build-up on fans, causing the machine to overheat. He went on to mention the failing batteries, which had nothing to do with computers as they were self-contained. They should be unaffected regardless of any build-up of dust.

It was the coincidences of the report that the public should not be told of in case it caused widespread panic.

The report finished leaving more questions than answers.

"Dust, what dust?" It was the first David had heard of it, and what about the batteries he had that were going flat, did this dust have something to do with that? By the time the General returned David was full of questions and the General knew it.

"Well, Major, what do you think?" the General asked gruffly.

"Well, Sir, I have a lot of questions," David replied straightforwardly.

The General smiled knowingly. "Yes, so did I after the meeting with the President, yet there are no real answers. Is the dust somehow interfering with both the computers and the batteries? I don't know, nor do I know how the public are going to handle the problem."

David was confused as to what was going on. Why was he here in the first place and what was he expected to do? He couldn't see his role in the coming crisis.

The General spoke quietly as if someone was listening. “Here’s what I require of you.” He paused a moment as if gathering his thoughts. “I want you to gather a team together and investigate what is happening.”

Taken aback by the unexpected request, David stammered, “Sir, surely there’s a scientist on staff that is better qualified for the task?”

The General looked perplexed. “That’s an order, Major,” he barked sharply then as quickly a smile came across his face. “Look, son,” he again said quietly, “you’re the only man I can trust, all the rest are in on the plot.”

Now it was David’s turn to look perplexed. “What plot is that, Sir?” David asked, all the time thinking that the General had lost the plot.

“You know what plot; this dust is just a plot by our enemies.” The General was angry now, almost out of control.

David thought it was time he got himself out of the situation and told the General that he had better go and collect his team. The General agreed, allowing David to go, however on the way out he put his hand on David’s shoulder.

“Trust no one, not even your wife, they’re all in it together.”

David was confused. What should he do? The man had obviously gone mad but who do you report a general to? He was still mulling over the problem when two hours later the word came through that the General had died. This was a new phase to the dust. It would build up in people and soon they started to die, their bodies drained of power like the batteries. It was dispersed across the globe and the scientists couldn’t work out why.

The dust was building up a little more every day and it increased as time went on. By then most batteries had failed and mainstream power was being affected. People were dying by the thousands. It was no longer an isolated and dispersed issue; it was becoming a global crisis.

Then there came widespread food shortages as the trucks stopped delivering. Power was intermittent and food riots started as people became desperate. They raided shopping centres and warehouses. The police force became powerless to quell the riots with their increasing frequency and most of them stayed at home to look after the own families.

The army was tied down by the lack of transport and they also abandoned their posts in search of food. Society was quickly becoming unstable as people scrambled to stay alive in the troubled times.

Then the personal violence started as gangs of men invaded homes searching for anything that would keep them going. Worldwide there was a mass exodus into the countryside. Battles were fought over the best recourses. That was in the future, for now John was defending his family; unlike most other people, he had access to firearms so he was in the position to drive the raiders away. Night time was worse as hungry people finding the supermarkets empty tried desperately to find food. Several times people had come to his door begging for help but he turned them away.

Luckily they didn't know he had stored food, otherwise they wouldn't have gone so easily. "Couldn't we spare a little food?" Ann asked as a mother and daughter walked away.

John sighed deeply. He couldn't, he knew he couldn't, his family depended on him being strong and the supplies staying in his hands. "You know that that can't happen," he said gently, "we're going to need all the food we have; we cannot afford to help other people." Locking eyes with Ann, John knew she would argue further.

"But…" Ann protested. "What's the use of being the only three alive and having all this food?"

In a tone as rigid as granite, John continued, "I want this family to survive, I'm sorry if I'm being a hard ass but other people will have to survive the best way they can."

Ann was very emotional and didn't mind letting John know it. "I can understand what you say but it's not fair to treat people this way."

John felt bad about the entire situation but was not about to change the way he was running things, his family was everything to him and he would do anything for their survival.

They withdrew into their own world as the world crumbled around them; the lights grew dim, and then went out altogether. The world went dark and candles along with gas became the only source of light. People lit fires and huddled around not for warmth but for security.

House raids became more frequent as time went on. Neighbours teamed up to protect their neighbourhoods, pitch battles were fought over a few supplies. This was in the early days and people were starting to drift from the city. John watched as his neighbours slowly drifted away. It upset him to see them go but he realised that they had to do it, their own survival depended on it.

One night John woke to the sound of breaking glass; for a moment he lay there listening then quickly slipped out of bed and retrieved his police pistol. As silently as he could he headed towards the front of the house.

There were three of them in the lounge room, they had not yet found anything. John had the advantage of knowing the layout of the house and slipped into the darkened room.

"You boys lost your way?" he said as the three froze on the spot. "I'm armed and ready to use it!" he said harshly, trying to make himself seem mean.

"So am I," came a voice from the darkness, "so you had better put your weapon down before I shoot you." The man's voice had a slight tremor to it and John felt his nervousness. "Drop your weapon," the man insisted again. "Drop it or I'll shoot."

John didn't know what to think, he didn't know if the man was armed or not, yet he didn't know if he should call him on it. A gun battle was the last thing he wanted in his home but on the other hand he couldn't let the men take what they wanted.

"I'm not joking I will shoot you." The man sounded desperate and afraid, as if his bluff wasn't working and he didn't know what to do about it. There was a movement to the side of the room as if someone was trying to outflank him. John realised he couldn't best three men if they decided to rush him so turning to the movement he fired his pistol.

There was a scream and the sound of a body dropping to the floor followed by a sobbing moan.

"Jesus Christ, he shot Charley!" the voice shouted, followed by the popping report of a small calibre pistol, then another shot.

The first bullet hissed past John's ear, the second went wide. John's first thoughts went to Ann and where she was; hopefully she had stayed in the bedroom but knowing her she would have gone to Devina's room. There was movement in front of him so he fired again, and there was another scream but no falling body.

"Son of a bitch!"a voice exclaimed, obviously in pain.

"Frank! You hurt, Frank?" The voice came from the darkness.

"Shut up, Vic," Frank barked angrily. "He can tell where you are." The man sounded in pain but still capable of fighting. John zeroed in on his voice and fired, there came a grunt and the sound of a body falling.

John's police pistol training was coming useful as all his shots had hit their target and there was only the gunman himself to deal with. He moved position, as he had each time he had fired but in doing so he had lost the location of the gunman. It seemed hours had gone by but in truth it had been less than thirty minutes. The longer the standoff went on the more he worried about his family. Ann had been taught not to get involved in the action no matter what and John hoped that training would keep her from harm.

"Mister, can we talk?" The voice had a whine about it.

John said nothing, not wanting to give his position away.

"Mister, I don't want to fight you anymore." Fear now clearly heard in the voice. "I'm putting my gun down, Mister." There was a metallic clunk as the firearm hit the tiles and the voice came again. "Please don't shoot me, Mister."

John was in two minds. To let the man live was to invite trouble later on, but to kill so cold bloodedly was not in his nature. The choice was confusing and he hesitated. The gunman must have taken his inaction as a sign that he wouldn't be killed and the sound of movement came to John's ears. The decision was made in the time it takes to pull a trigger. Locating the sound, John fired; he couldn't take any chance with his family's safety on the line.

"Oh shit!" came the final words from the darkness, then a thud as a body hit the floor. John wasn't sure if he had wounded the man or killed him outright. No sound came from the man so John took it as a clean kill.

The sun was a long time in rising; finally John was able to see the night's slaughter. Three men were dead and blood had pooled under their bodies. He felt sick at what he had done but realised that there had been no other choice. There was an intake of air behind him and he realised that Ann was standing there.

"My God, John, are you alright?" With a voice stretched thin by tension she struggled with the scene before her.

He turned to her. "There was no other way," he explained, his voice thick with guilt.

Ann took him into her arms and whispered, "I know."

It took several hours to bury the bodies in the corner of the back garden away from the vegetable plot then two more hours to clean the blood from the tiles using water from the rain water tanks.

Out in the city things were getting worse. People were dying from the dust interfering with their bodies' electrical system and there was no one to collect the bodies. Horses became the main transport and steam trains were put back into service, but the lack of water towers stopped the trains from being any use. Besides the trains' limited usefulness there was nothing in the way of food being manufactured for the trains to haul.

The army took over the remaining bulk food storage with their families. They weren't really willing to share the food with mere civilians, as many people found out, usually through a savage beating or outright murder when they tried to get at it.

Everything failed; power, water and gas. The gas lasted for longer than any of the other utilities. Dogs and cats started to disappear from the streets as hunger became more prevalent and the city started to smell of rotten corpses.

People were on the move into the countryside. Where sheep and cattle still ran free, farmers tried in vain to keep their livestock safe, but were quickly overrun by the hungry hordes. Packs of ghoulish, poverty-stricken people would clean out all the animals from one farm and move onto the next with no thought for their fellows nor the future. Country towns put up a defence but the hordes moved around them, isolating the towns with little food and the farms stripped of anything edible.

To Eric Fanbridge and his wife Liza their hobby farm was their life. They had been on it for over twenty years; they ran a few cattle and sheep. Other than this small herd of livestock they had an extensive vegetable garden and their only source of power was solar and wind turbines, both of which now didn't work. They had adjusted to life without power very quickly, cleaning out the fridge and freezer. Gas lights and candles took electricity's place and they had hens for eggs and food. They were in a good position to survive in comfort until the horde arrived, then everything changed. Finally they were left with nothing that could be eaten. Then the horde moved off leaving them with little except what food they had been able hide. Yet all was not lost, there was seed they hadn't planted and fruit that was still developing on the trees. It would be tight but they could survive. And for meat there were dozens of kangaroos in the bush.

For John the days went slowly. He spent time in the vegetable garden watering each individual plant as water was short; there was not enough to shower but a bucket full to wash down twice a week did the job. There had been no more trouble from looters and John felt safe enough to leave his family and go searching for food to supplement their supplies. Most of the time he was unsuccessful yet sometimes a small supply of food and other goods was discovered. There were still people about and John made sure they didn't follow him home. He had found two boxes of dog food at the back of a nearby supermarket when a young woman approached him.

"Please, sir, can you give me something to eat?" she begged.

John for some reason took pity on the girl and handed over two large cans of the dog food. "Now go away," he said sharply. The girl cringed and hugging her cans to her chest started to back away with fear in her eyes. John felt sorry for the girl, two cans wouldn't last her long and there was little else edible to be found. Still his family came first as always. He was extra cautious on the way home, always aware of his surroundings. It wasn't until he got home did he feel any remorse. He had condemned the girl to a slow death by starvation and for the first time he questioned his ideas about family first.

The days turned into weeks, and as the weeks went by they too began to blend into months until finally the food ran out and John had the choice to try and live off the vegetable garden or go on the road to search for a better place. In the end there was only one choice to make, for owing to the shortage of water they had to move. The day came quickly and with backpacks full of their remaining food they left their home. Heading into the unknown they were well aware that as they hadn't wanted to share their food with anyone, it was unlikely that anyone would want to share with them.

By now the hordes had run their course. Starvation had taken its toll, leaving few to carry on. In eight months the population had dropped by a stagging seventy five per cent and the rest now lived a subsistence existence, hunting and fishing. Farming was coming back though far too slowly with the few animals left as breed stock. Wheat was sown by hand in small plots and fruit gathered from abandoned orchards. This was the new world that John and his family found themselves in and to John's surprise the whole family found themselves welcomed into the small community.

"How did it happen so fast?" John asked Peter, the leader of the group. "I expected it to last for years before it got to this level."

A forlorn look came over Peter's face as he relived the previous few months. "It happened fast. Most people were city dwellers and didn't know how to look after themselves once the easy food was gone. They couldn't hunt or fish and once winter hit they starved very quickly."

Disbelievingly John continued to question. "But so many so quickly? I'm surprised they didn't last longer."

"The worst part was getting rid of the bodies," Peter explained. "There are camps where the bodies haven't been disposed of."

John was puzzled after seeing the order of the camp when they were first welcomed in. “But I thought you had everything under control.”

Peter pointed towards the palisade surrounding the camp. “No, far from it, there are mobs of people still roaming the countryside attacking the villages. We have to fight to keep what’s ours and to protect ourselves.”

John and his family had not seen any of the roaming mobs during their flight into the country. “But you let me in without hesitation. Don’t I pose a threat?”

Peter laughed. “I’m a good judge of character, I can tell if a person will be good for the village or not.”

John was satisfied with the answer and realised that he and his family could be happy in the village and on his part working the land. If it came to a fight he was willing and able. For those remaining in the mobs it was a matter of adapt or die out. Villages became stronger in their defences and more willing to shoot first and ask questions later. Slowly those roaming the countryside settled down and became less of a threat to people around them. Life stabilised to the slow rhythm of the seasons and John found out that life on the land was hard but satisfying. He learned all the natural remedies to take the place of manufactured drugs. Tanned hides slowly replaced clothing. Even though there were plenty of clothes in the cities, to get at them meant days riding on horseback or longer on foot.

The return to the middle ages was complete within two years of the dust’s arrival. In some places steam was being used but only for minor reasons. Still the steam age had a chance to return if only after many years.

To John and his family, life after dust, or L.A.D as it was known, became easier as time went by. Small towns became trading posts and doctors appeared on the scene. Life in general became more tolerable and within ten years horse travel was normal.

Within twenty years they had the railways re-established and man was back to the pioneer days. Things were easier to build the second time around and people had the will to learn past skills.

Life had, once again become worthwhile.

FINDING THE SPARK

Nicolas Massu

Peter was at home and on TV he started to watch a documentary on the Discovery Channel where he learned how ancient people lived. The program explained that when they were born they learned to use rocks to get a spark to light fires. Peter was so fascinated about that that he wanted to have the rocks to himself and experience what it was like at that time; like seeing dinosaurs in real life. Excitedly Peter grabbed two rocks that were of grey colour but when he struck them together, much to his dismay and disappointment there was no spark. Peter was so anxious to get the spark out of the rocks. He was yearning to find out what two rocks would get a spark. Peter knew it would take time though in his eagerness his impatience became apparent. Peter became frantic, telling his friends constantly that when he grew up and went camping he would use those rocks and live the life that our ancestors lived without thinking of using a lighter or a match, excited to live his own story of survival.

Peter's family wasn't rich and his dad had to work really hard to get money. His dad was named Marcelo and was always working really hard, so much so that he had little time for family matters. Marcelo also needed to provide food for his family and so whatever Peter was thinking was seen to be nonsense because Marcelo had no time for childish things. Marcelo found out that if he studied geology he might be able to work at the mines.

"Just think about it," Marcelo was saying to himself, "if I work at the mines I would really provide for my family." Marcelo wasn't thinking about how he could have a meaningful and decent life for his family; he knew that money was what people wanted, so Marcelo focused only on this. For Peter though, this was a great chance to find out what rocks get a spark when they are struck.

One day Peter was asking Marcelo unending questions about minerals and rocks, however Marcelo was too busy studying and working to spend time helping Peter. So Peter decided to go to a mine site and ask other people, people who would have time for him. However Peter did not know how he was going to do that if he could not get there and also, how was he going to get inside the mine company and get the two rocks?

Peter's mum Olivia was concerned about Peter because his dad wasn't spending much time with him; she was worried Peter would end up doing something that they would all later regret. Olivia decided to speak to Marcelo and ask whether or not it would be feasible for her to work so that Marcelo could spend some time with Peter. However Marcelo said, "Let Peter grow up and do not ask those kinds of questions." Marcelo was interested about money, not spending time with his son because he was the man of this house and if he could provide enough to get video games then Peter would be happy.

Peter overheard the conversation but he still wanted the rocks. A year had passed and Peter was in high school. He decided to do physics to find his rock. The physics teacher, Carlos, told Peter that his class would not be discussing such things. However Carlos said if Peter learnt about the periodic table he might be able to find out about the elements and the rock compositions. Peter liked the idea but he was still so focused on finding the two rocks, right now. Peter was anxious and impatient; he wanted those rocks now, not tomorrow. Peter's obsession was why Olivia thought that he was developing some sort of illness, drawing her own conclusions from how little time Marcelo spent with him.

Olivia took Peter to see a paediatrician and the doctor said that Peter might be developing a form of ADHD. Before confirming this the paediatrician said he needed to run some tests. First he wanted to know how much concentration Peter had and how well he did at school. Then he ran the Wechsler Adult Intelligence Scale test as he thought that Peter would benefit from that, but as he was under eighteen it would not be definitive. Being subjected to the tests, Peter began to believe that he might have an illness and therefore must be drugged. That was a huge set-back for him, he felt stigma for the first time, thinking, "Who wants to be with a person who has to take medication?" and no matter what, people were going to treat him as a disabled kid.

Peter was given the medication Dexamphetamine and thought it would fix his problems. His belief in medication was shaken when he was told, "Medication doesn't give life skills." Peter carried on, going to school and he kept quiet about his Dexamphetamine but the teacher had to know. Telling Carlos about this let some school mates overhear the conversation; then the bullying began with them saying, "You are sick." Peter decided then that no matter what, he wasn't going to give up.

Days passed and Peter was getting more in depth into physics. One day Carlos was talking about nuclear physics and Peter was excited. For the first time he was learning about the elements. Carlos wanted to send his students to an upcoming physics exhibition but Peter didn't know if he would be invited. Peter tried his hardest to be able to go but because of his ADHD he wasn't able to learn at the same pace as his classmates.

Carlos pulled Peter aside after class. "I'm sorry, Peter, but you can't go to the exhibition, your grades aren't good enough". Carlos could see Peter's disappointment and said, "If you want to go next time, study, be prepared and keep your interest keen. You need to move past this obsession with the rock."

Peter understood but was still not going to give up. He knew that the teacher was telling the truth and deep down knew he was only doing physics to find that rock. Peter knew things must change in order for him to be able to get what he wanted and also knew he could achieve success in everything he wanted to do if he gave up the obsession. The funny thing is, obsessions aren't ruled by logic.

Peter knew that in his country he had to enlist in the army after finishing school and this time was fast approaching. Before he commenced compulsory service Peter sold some of his ADHD medication, getting enough to pay for a bus to go to a nearby mine site and get his two rocks. Peter got $100 and he was happy with it, waiting for Saturday when his mum would let him spend time with his friends.

He got up really early that Saturday and said to his mum, "Bye, Mum, I'm off to see Oswald."

Olivia knew that it was too early for Peter to see his friends, but she trusted him and let him go. Olivia said, “You can play with Oswald at the arcade but be back before the evening comes.”

Meeting up with Oswald, a glint of mischievousness flickering in their eyes, they went to the bus station and hopped on a bus headed to Showcase Town, the closest place to the mine site. You can imagine the excitement of Peter and Oswald as they were travelling there, they just couldn’t wait. One hour later they arrived and wandered around for a half an hour asking people how to get to the Crested Crown mine. Someone told them to get to the mine company you needed to drive because the bus only went there three times a week and the next one was Monday. Peter and Oswald were overcome with disappointment, however they found a villager who offered to take them there but he would not be able to take them back. The excitement returned as Peter and Oswald didn’t care if they couldn’t get back on the same day. Only caring about the rocks, they went along with it. The villager told them who to speak to at the mine company to get information on the rocks that Peter wanted to have. The villager left them at the mine’s entrance wishing them luck.

Peter and Oswald went to the office and asked the first person they met if they could talk about the rock.

The receptionist said, “I’m sorry, young man, I’m new to Crested Crown and don’t know what rocks we really have here.”

Peter and Oswald told him what they had to go through to get to the mine company. As they expressed their disappointment a man wearing a dust-covered business suit and PPE walked in. Walking up to the counter, he gruffly asked, “What is it that those kids want?”

The receptionist replied, “They want to know about rocks and see which ones sparked.”

Then the suited man asked the boys, “Why do you kids want to know that?”

Peter said, clearly passionate “I just find myself fascinated about how our ancestors were using those rocks to create fire, sir.” Then he added, “I went to all the trouble to ask my dad, who is studying geology, and I am doing physics and came to the mine company just for this, sir. I might get in trouble with my mum because we can’t even return home tonight, but I don’t care, I’m sure I’ll find those rocks here.”

The man looked upon the boys kindly. “My name is Daniel and I am the manager of Crested Crown. The rocks you are looking for are quartz and you can find them anywhere on this site.” Turning his back on the boys briefly, Daniel went through some papers behind the desk before handing them to Peter. “I love your passion, son, if your father has one tenth of that I want him to work for us. Have him fill out these papers and give me a call. By the way, I just happen to have two pieces of quartz in my office that you can have as a souvenir.” Walking away with a wink, Daniel said over his shoulder, “I’ll just go grab them and give you a lift back into town so you don’t get into too much trouble.”

Peter found the rocks at last and with Daniel’s help had gotten home just after nightfall. When they got into the city it was 7 p.m. and Peter wanted to tell his mum about the adventure, but knew telling her would cause too much trouble.

Olivia asked him, “How did you go today, Peter?”

He said, “Fine but I have to confess something.”

Olivia said, “And what’s that?”

Peter couldn’t suppress his guilty smile. “We went to Showcase Town and into Crested Crown.”

Olivia didn’t know what to say or figure out how she was going to punish Peter. Frustrated, she said, “Just wait until Dad gets home, he can punish you.”

Marcelo came home at 8:30pm and Peter told him what Daniel had said, handing him the paperwork. He told Marcelo that he had been offered a job at the mine site and his dad replied, “Thanks, son. I should have listened to you from the beginning. If this works out the family will be taken care of and I can pay more attention to you.”

Peter was overcome with his accomplishment and from that day forward Peter’s family lived a happy life.

MCFLY SAVES THE DAY

Nicolas Massu

Chile is renowned as a place where there are lots of earthquakes. One sunny day the children at school count down the days of the remaining school year. Today is safety awareness day. The kids are taken through the evacuation process and told where the assembly area is in case of an earthquake.

It is said by many people that there is a way of knowing when an earthquake will strike and one of them is by listening to dogs when they howl. When dogs howl they are being alerted by a frequency deep underground. This frequency is the earthquake; it vibrates and creates sound waves. When the sound reaches the dogs they howl because their ears are affected and they are hurt. As with any living thing in pain they express themselves, so the dogs do not have a choice but to howl.

Dogs can bark too, however in this instance they do not because their ears are affected and that lasts until the vibrations of the earthquake stop.

In the little suburb of La Herradura there is a primary school where the school warden is in charge of alerting the school kids to assemble in case of a possible earthquake. The school does an earthquake drill at least twice every year and that gives the students the chance to prepare for what is involved.

The school warden has a satellite phone that can connect to the emergency services in Santiago de Chile called ONEMI. Satellite phones are necessary because the phone lines could be down or the wires cut. This way they can always connect to ONEMI and wait for further instructions.

The warden from time to time reassures the students that the classrooms are safe and secure, promising that an earthquake will not break the walls. The warden then tells the students of each classroom what the procedure is for each of them to do.

First the students are to go under their desks. Then they are to form two lines, one for the boys and one for the girls. Then they are to go with the teacher to the emergency assembly area.

One sunny day in September the warden conducts an emergency evacuation drill. Everything goes well and the school warden is well pleased. The next evacuation that year is in winter, and this is the worst winter for many years due to a drought. Dogs in winter feel the chill weather intensely and do not waste time barking, lest they lose their voice.

One day during that winter, McFly is the only dog in La Herradura barking, and then he howls. That however is not reason enough for other dogs to howl; it is raining and the other dogs are not as sensitive as him and not affected as much. McFly is a dog that is very caring and loves helping people.

As it happens a tremor comes registering a magnitude of five on the Richter scale. The school warden sounds the alarm. The students do not like this.

“Fancy calling a drill on a day like today,” they think. It is raining and they do not want to get wet.

Then many dogs start howling to alert people of a possible earthquake. It is then that a magnitude eight earthquake strikes La Herradura.

After the tremors subside and life returns to normal McFly receives the merit of honor from the local government for alerting people about an earthquake.

FRENCH HOLIDAY

Arri R. Taieb

I awoke to feel zee warmth of zee morning sun streaming across me, warming my vitals. Opening my eye I squinted up at my master who lay `ap`azardly across zee bed, arms and legs flung out in drunken abandon where `e `ad collapsed zee night before. I needed to pee and `oped `e would wake up soon to let me go. I moved with some discomfort and in doing so disturbed and woke `eem. `E let out a pleasurable groan and shifted `eez body into zee longest, most luxurious stretch that seemed to go on and on and on. Suddenly, `e leapt from zee bed calling to me, "Come on, Stumpy, I know what you want," and opened zee door for me. Later, watching `eem shave in zee bathroom with zee window open and gentle breezes bringing in all zee delightful aromas of zee springtime, I couldn't `elp but notice zee open window of zee opposite chalet. Every time zee breeze lifted zee lacy curtain I could see a woman in `er shower. I stood up to get a better look and my master noticed my movement. "Down, boy," `e said, "we've got plenty of time; we're here for anozzer week at least".

`Owever, zat didn't stop `eem from taking anozzer look at ze beautiful dusky form soaping `erself in all `er glorious nakedness. As soon as `e `ad fineeshed `iz ablutions `e was out zee door and off down to zee beach to take an early morning swim, whistling to me as `e went. "C'mon, Stumpy, race you to zee beach." On reaching zee ocean `e took an almighty lunge and dove beneath zee waves. Powering `eemself out to zee floating platform anchored for swimmers `e `auled `eemself out to sunbathe. `E stretched `eemself out and soaked up zee sunshine. `Alf an hour later `e was back in zee water and `eading for zee beach and breakfast.

Breakfast was a fairly laid-back non-event with a couple of "Bon Jours" exchanged `ere and there but I could see that my master was on zee lookout for zee dusky maiden of zee chalet next-door. I lay down in zee shade and decided to keep an eye open for `er as well. Unfortunately for my master she was a no-show at breakfast and it wasn't until early evening just as we were going in to dinner zat we caught sight of `er waiting to be seated in zee dining room. My master rudely pushed `eemself to zee front of zee queue and boldly took `er elbow to steer `er to a table for two at zee back of zee restaurant. Dinner was a fantastic affair, zey `it it off instantly and you could almost touch zee animal magnetism between zee two of zem.

"Zo, why a natureest colony?" `e asked.

"Well, when we were children my mama and papa would always take us to zee natureest beaches for zee summer `olidays and I `ave nevair forgotten zat incredible feeling of freedom and `appiness; so whenever I can I try to recapture `eet," she breathed `uskily. "What about you?"

"Well, when we were children my mama and papa would nevair take us to zee natureest beaches for zee summer `olidays and I `ave nevair forgotten zat incredible feeling of restriction and sadness so whenever I can I try to experience eet," `e answered laughingly.

After dinner zey took zeir cocktails and went out onto zee terrace where zee brilliance of zee moon was caught in `er glorious `air, rippling like a silvery river over `er shoulders and cascading down `er back. My master was entranced. "Come back to my chalet weeth me," `e whispered in `er ear and gently took `er elbow to guide `er back through zee restaurant.

As zey passed through, zee music from zee band attracted `er attention and she nuzzled `is `ear. "I would love to dance," she murmured. `E guided her onto zee dance floor and `eld `er in a tight embrace while I settled down to just keeping an eye open.

Over zee next `alf hour or so I was content to let zem caress necks and shoulders and whisper all manner of sweet nuzzings but I became instantly alert as `e surreptitiously guided `er toward zee door and out again into zee moonlight. Zey `eld each other tightly as zey stumbled along zee winding villa pathways, laughing and giggling like silly teenagers until zey arrived at `is chalet; zen fumbled zeir way into zee bedroom tearing each ozzer's clothes off and falling `elplessly across zee bed. It was at zis point zat I decided to take part in zee action and zee dusky beauty was very obliging. Two minutes later I was totally worn out and shrank back into my cosy, damp nest, exhausted but very `appy.

Oh! I am so rude. Please forgive moi! I forgot to introduce myself. I am

M'sieur Stumpy L'Appendage, Esquire.

HER RELEASE

Matthew Nicholson

As the string is tightly wound,
I can see the pleasure written across her face.
Slowly blood rushes to the mound,
And her heart begins to pace.
So hot, she feels her face flush,
Waves of pleasure, of pain.
Oh the excitement, it's been too long, the rush,
With nothing to lose and all to gain.
Soon she'll be lost within the feeling,
As wave upon wave it begins to mount.
It's now almost too hard to focus, and soon she won't be dealing,
This will be a story too embarrassing to recount.
I hope at the end it won't cause a dimple,
As she pops that painful pimple.

LOSS

Matthew Nicholson

Deborah laid the roses across the glossy walnut wood that made his tiny casket, the pale pink of their velvet soft petals contrasting starkly against both the sombre grey wood and the shattered, razor edges that were her feelings today. Deborah thought to herself, "Today is not a day for soft feelings and pretty things." Even inside her own head Deborah could not remove the catch in her throat, or the bitter contempt she felt for herself in letting this happen. Tears began to well in her beautiful sapphire eyes, dulling their usual crystalline brilliance. Try as she might the flood gates could not be held any longer, and like the thoroughbred stallions at Ascot, once one tear had broken free the stampede could not be contained. Lines of diluted black mascara raced down Deborah's cheeks, their normal flawless porcelain now blotched with irregular pink patterns denoting her distress.

Deborah turned her back on that little wooden box and walked back to her place by her mother's side. Leaving him, the walk itself seemed to drag on into eternity, as if walking down a darkened tunnel with but a single pinpoint of light to guide your step. However for Deborah, with his passing, that light had been extinguished, each step harder and more precarious to take.

Once at her mother's side Deborah looked upon a woman, so unmoved it appeared as if she were carved from stone. So stolid in the face of tragedy; the granite stare, steady breathing and solidity of form... this was what it meant to be the woman of the house. She was the foundation for the family, the stalwart pillar which held up those around her. This was a role Deborah would one day need to fill. Deborah knew she would soon need to be strong when others could not; however today, today was not that day. Deborah shied away from her mother's unyielding stare, turning; a stolen moment of solitude and a last instant for her to let the feelings fall freely fragments of shattered glass, each memory jagged and cutting.

With a glance at her mother's face, Deborah could easily see the mounting impatience for her prolonged emotional release. She knew she could not put off her final words any longer. Her mother then made the first movement Deborah had registered all day, moving in closely to her right ear and saying simply, "It's time." The words shocked Deborah from her reverie of misery; her mother's voice gravelly, coarse, and grating against the paper-thin veneer Deborah was failing to maintain.

By now the sun had begun to set. The barren limbs of the old oak trees were stark against the crimson sky on this winter's day. The movement of the sun across the sky set the shadows of those limbs dancing. A bizarre and macabre dance, seemingly timed and choreographed, but set to no earthly music. Slowly, the shadows coalesced with what seemed a singular and cognisant purpose. Shadowy fingers extended toward the coffin, now so seemingly tiny compared to the sinister darkness creeping to embrace it. As the outstretched fingers touched the tiny wooden box a strong gust of wind buffeted both trees and mourning party from the south west. The frigid wind added a physical coldness to the pervasive emotional bitterness of the day. With the sudden onset of the wind, the shadowy dance increased its tempo; fingers of pitch lapped, laced and interlocked, appearing as if the shadows themselves beckoned, encouraging him to join them in their depthless darkness.

Drawing a long, faltering breath, Deborah prepared herself to deliver the eulogy she had practised innumerable times these last two days. "Today is a sad day for us all. We are brought here to bid farewell to one very dear to us. Iggy has been taken from us far too soon, though isn't that always the way, for the kindest amongst us?"

Deborah continued her heartfelt speech, pouring out emotion bottled up since the day she had found Iggy's cold, lifeless form. She retold favourite memories, reliving in her mind and the minds of all in attendance the good times, moments of light-hearted joy and the way things used to be. Finally, Deborah's deliverance drew to a close. "Iggy, I and all those here today will always remember you. Broken now, our hearts will heal, and though scarred by your passing, forever will you be with us."

Deborah fell quiet, moving to join her mother by the side of Iggy's coffin. Together, they bore that dreadful weight. He was so slight in her hands but heavy on her soul. For Deborah each step toward the grave dug earlier that day was a tolling of Iggy's death knell. Lowering that tiny, yet ever so significant box into the earth was hard, harder than Deborah had imagined it would be. She had said her goodbyes, but in her actions there was a finality that even Deborah could not refute.

With the first shovel full of soil the veneer Deborah had set in place peeled away, and her tears began anew. Slowly the earth piled up until the only sign of Iggy's existence was the discolouration of the recently disturbed dirt.

Stepping back to her mother's side Deborah noticed how even that patch of upturned soil blended into the greater surrounds. "Is this all there is? Does life lead to nothing but death and left behind sorrows?" Deborah asked aloud, not expecting an answer. Time seemed to pass slowly as Deborah was lost to her musings on the meaning of life.

Her mother then turned to her and said, "Come inside, Debbie, the service is finished and we need to get ready for when your father returns home."

Deborah couldn't move from where she stood and just shook her head in response to her mother. Turning red-rimmed eyes back to staring at the spot where Iggy had gone, Deborah let her tears flow unashamedly. Deborah's mother let out an almost inaudible sigh before moving forward to Deborah's side, placing a hand upon her right shoulder. Imparting as much false sympathy into her voice as she could, she left Deborah with some final words. "Debbie, Iggy was a good boy and we will all miss him. Stay out here for as long as you need and once your father gets home I'll talk to him. When you're ready I'll get him to come and speak to you; maybe he'll let us go into town to get you a new iguana tomorrow."

LOST

Raymond L. Henderson

The rain beat steadily on the windscreen as the swish of the wipers broke the silence. David had been on the road for more than twelve hours and weariness was showing. Around him the rain-filled night fought his headlights, making it hard to distinguish the road ahead. David realised that he should have stopped at the motel five hours before when the sun had set and the weather had moved in. The sense of urgency that had made him carry on was now a distant memory as frustration set in. All he needed was a hot meal, an equally hot shower and a good night's sleep.

He yawned and rubbed his eyes, wondering as he did whether he should pull up in the next truck bay and get some sleep. He discounted the idea and decided that the next garage diner couldn't be too far away. He checked his fuel gauge, A quarter full, that was a worry but according to the road sign at the motel he should have been there by now. He turned on the radio but was rewarded with nothing but static so he switched to a CD instead. Music instantly drove the silence away and made David feel a lot better.

The country music seemed to put a buffer between him and the rain-drenched Australian bush. It was at this time that he saw a sign saying, “Rapid River Truck Stop 12 kilometres ahead”. David was elated. The thought of a hot meal made his mouth water. Outside the rain had eased slightly, which made driving easier and he was able to speed up. Finally the garage came into sight, an island of light surrounded by an ocean of darkness. David slowed to enter the driveway and rolled to a stop at the bowsers. There were several cars in the parking lot but no one to be seen.

Slamming the car into park, he pulled up the handbrake and alighted. He tried to fill his tank but the bowsers never came on. Grumpily he headed inside to find the reason why, only to be greeted with dead silence and an empty garage. Puzzled, he rang the bell on the counter and waited, the only relief from the graveyard silence the distant sound of the garage’s generator. Puzzlement shifted into uneasiness as he headed back behind the counter. The kitchen was empty as were the staff rooms. He explored further and found the entire garage empty. He then headed to the motel rooms, knocking on each door in turn. There was no reply, no sleepy mumble, no shouted abuse, nothing to his persistent knocking.

David was confused, where the hell was everyone? It was like everyone had packed up and left, leaving their cars behind. David’s stomach growled and he headed into the restaurant to find food. After he had eaten from the buffet, whose food was still fresh and tasty, he headed into the kitchen to turn off the stove in case it started a fire. Walking back to the main desk he surveyed the vacancy board and then, selecting a key from the key board, and turned in for the night.

The next morning was as rain soaked as the night before. He made his way to the kitchen, looking around as he did. Nothing had changed, the place was still deserted. In the kitchen he turned on the stove and cooked himself a hearty meal and pondered as he was eating. He walked outside under the garage patio and looked into the bush that surrounded the garage. It went on like this as far as the eye could see; low shrubs to the horizon, here and there a stunted tree. It was wet and miserable and he felt the same. It was then that he realised he had to get out of there.

It took a while for him to work out how to start the self service equipment at the bowsers but once he did he filled his car. Without looking back he drove off down a rain-soaked road. The day went quickly as he pushed the car to the maximum speed limit, which ate the kilometres up. The afternoon drifted into evening and darkness slowly engulfed the road ahead. A few kangaroos bounded across the road forcing him to slow down. Finally after ten hours on the road he saw a sign for a roadhouse ahead: Rapid River Truck Stop 12 kilometres. David was more than surprised and instantly overcome with wariness and suspicion.

Twelve kilometres later he pulled into the same garage that he had left that morning. The only difference was that another car was pulled up at the bowsers. As he alighted from his vehicle a woman came out of the building, confusion written clearly across her face.

“Thank God you’re here,” she exclaimed. “There’s no one here and we were starting to worry.”

He looked the woman over. We? She was blonde, medium height and about forty. “I know,” he said flatly, the shock of being back at Rapid River still in his system.

“You know what?” the woman asked, her voice becoming shrill with frustration and fear.

David shook his head to clear his mind. “I’m sorry, I meant to say that I know about no one being here.”

The woman looked more confused than ever. “How did you know?”

Briefly David explained what had happened and to his surprise the woman took it well. “I’m David,” he managed to say as two teenage girls walked out of the building.

“Marie,” she said, “and my daughters Kristine, fifteen and Diane, thirteen.” She added their ages as if it were important and to her it probably was. “Where do we go from here?” she asked, strangely calm after speaking with him.

“We try again tomorrow and see if we can get to another garage.” He didn’t bring up what they would do if they couldn’t; it was something that he didn’t want to contemplate until he had no other choice.

The evening went well. Over a meal they got to know each other better and by the time they retired for the night, they felt comfortable in each other’s company. Breakfast was early as David wanted to leave as soon as possible. As the rain had eased he felt they could make good time. At noon they stopped for a rest, to allow everyone to stretch their legs and answer the call of nature. After the break they set off again.

It was late afternoon when David saw the Rapid River sign and his heart sank. Gripping the steering wheel tighter he couldn’t suppress the despondent thought, “Was there no way out of this endless cycle that they seemed to be in?”

Pulling into the garage… again, he could see his own despondency mirrored on Marie's face as she alighted from her vehicle. The despair and hopelessness she was feeling cloyed her very being.

"It seems we are in some sort of trap," David said, trying to keep his voice neutral.

"But how? What is happening? Why us?" Marie said shakily.

"I don't know, in fact I can't even understand what's going on or what we can do about it."

They went inside and as the girls were hungry they prepared a meal. Neither he nor Marie were hungry as worry had killed their appetites. After the meal the girls played games on their cell phones and the adults discussed their problem.

"Tomorrow we can try going back the way we came and see if that is any better," David suggested.

"Do you think it will be any use? Going back will probably give the same results. We're stuck here!" Marie's desperation to escape the inexplicable made her panicky.

"Maybe so, but we have to try. If we don't then we will just sit here until we run out of food or diesel for the generators. I don't know when the tanks were last filled." David was firm with her, taking on the role of the strong and stable man though he felt like crumbling himself. By the time they retired for the night they had talked for two hours. David had found out about Marie's marriage breakup and David let her see a glimpse into his life as a single man and career as a travelling salesman.

Early next morning they were on the road by eight o'clock and drove for four hours before having a break and drinking coffee from a thermos flask they had found. David looked around the bush. There was nothing unusual in their surroundings. He felt frustrated that there was nothing there; all he wanted was to see something strange, something to explain what was happening.

Ten hours after they left they found themselves back at the Rapid River station approaching from the opposite direction from where they had left. "It's as if the road goes in a large circle," David commented half to himself as he pondered the situation.

They were just settling down to a meal when the sound of a vehicle approaching brought them to their feet. They were outside in time to watch as the car slowly rolled to the bowsers. A woman alighted followed by two young teenage boys and they stood looking at David and his group.

"Hello," the woman said, "is there hot food available?"

David started responding to her as he approached. "Hello, we are just sitting down to a meal, I'm sure we can accommodate three extra."

Coming to a stop in front of David she began, "I'm Sue and these are my boys, Colin and Andrew."

David introduced the group and they went inside where over the course of the meal David and Marie explained the situation to Sue. At first she didn't want to accept the situation but as they talked they were able to convince her it was true. The next few days went by so slowly that everyone was soon fed up with each other. Some of the time was taken up doing a stock take of food and fuel. Much to David's dismay the overhead fuel tank feeding the generator was only a third full. As the main tank was not connected to the generator tank they couldn't expect the lights to stay on much longer and as most of the food was frozen or in the large cool room their perishables were in danger as well.

David was worried over the next few days as he racked his brain to find a way out of their problems or at least a way to delay the inevitable. Hand transferring fuel was a task that was daunting but achievable, yet this was only a temporary solution for the real problem: sooner or later they were going to run out of fuel.

It was four nights later that David slept the soundest sleep of his life. In the morning the others commented on how well they had slept and how well they were feeling and that feeling stayed with them all day. In the afternoon David went to check the generator tank to find out how much fuel they had used and to make a decision on when to start moving the fuel from the main tank. To his surprise the tank was full to the brim and after the shock had settled down he decided the two tanks were connected after all and the generator tank had filled automatically. This knowledge lifted a weight off his mind. At least they would not run out of power any time soon. Now he needed to focus on the food as it was the next to be depleted and the new big worry. Though he had seen kangaroos out in the bush he had no way of hunting them and no skill even if he had a way. There was nothing that could be done except ration the food and hope things sorted themselves out before they all starved to death.

The women understood the reason that they needed to ration their food but the logic was lost on the four hungry teenagers who thought that help was just around the corner. It took a while to make them understand that help may not be there when they needed it and they had no way of replenishing their supplies.

The days went by and David returned again and again to the generator tank to try and find the feed pipe from the main tank. He couldn't find one and that worried him. If the fuel didn't come from the main tank then where the hell did it come from? It remained a mystery that bugged David but one he kept to himself. There was no need to worry the women over something that must have a simple explanation. He put it to the back off his mind and concentrated on their supply issues.

Water was no problem as two huge water tanks were full with all the rain they had had over the past few days. Food was a different story. By his calculations they had enough to last them a month at most and that was with even stricter rationing. There was nothing that could be done except to try to break free of the loop that they had unwittingly found themselves in. He tried time and time again, leaving just after sunrise and arriving back ten hours later. No matter which way he went, the results were the same.

Boredom set in and David found himself spending more time walking in the bush on the few days that it didn't rain. The women cleaned, made beds and cooked to keep themselves occupied. The children played on the gaming machines that were to the side of the main restaurant. They spent hours feeding coins into the machines, retrieving the coins each day so they could keep on playing.

They were down to a few days' supplies when one night they felt extremely tired. Everyone retired early and they slept the night through, to wake next morning refreshed. After their showers they headed into the kitchen for breakfast. The first thing that hit David was that all the potato chip bags had been replaced and on further inspection all the food stores had also been restored. Even though some of the fruit and vegetables seemed strange most of it was recognisable. The meat also had a different look about it and the eggs had a light blue shell but the stocks were full and starvation seemed further away.

"What the hell happened last night?" Marie asked, bewildered at the change.

David's bewilderment was tempered by suspicion. "I don't know, this is as new to me as it is to you." His suspicion made his tone harsh.

"But it seems that all our needs are being met," Sue interrupted, also perplexed.

"It would seem so, this…" David said as he gestured to their new supply of food, "…and the fuel."

Crossing her arms Sue demanded, "The fuel? What about the fuel?"

Quickly David explained about the fuel appearing out of thin air and how he had sought a simple answer, but now it seemed that Sue was right they were being kept.

"But why? What could the reason for all this be?" Marie asked, her voice tense and shaky.

"If that's true then there is someone controlling all this, someone we can get in touch with, someone we can reason with," David said, trying to use logic to settle her.

"Reason with?" Marie spat, battling to hold the tears in. "How can you reason with someone that keeps you in a cage? It's like we're animals… yes that's it, we're in a zoo."

Marie was becoming frantic and David continued trying to stem the panic. "Take it easy, we don't know if that is true, there could be some logical explanation for all this." David didn't even believe his own placations; a zoo was the best explanation for their predicament.

David had been in an open range zoo and it described their situation to a tee. Though who could be behind this? And how did it work? Cameras? They must have cameras everywhere to keep an eye on things. Leaving the speculations for the moment they gave in to their hunger. Breakfast was more lavish than they had had in the past few days. Bacon, eggs, tomatoes, mushrooms and potato cakes filled their plates almost to overflow.

After they had cleaned up they sat down to discuss their predicament but try as they might no rational explanation came forth. They all agreed however that they were in some type of a holding area, which may or may not be a zoo. David went on a walk to try and clear his head and fill it with something, anything that made sense. His thoughts cascaded. How come they were the only ones here? Why hadn't anyone on the outside discovered a slice of Australia missing? Was it a government test? Were they trying to prove something? The questions went on and on until his mind could take no more. A kangaroo stood close by him and didn't move, knowing perhaps that David could do it no harm. How easily they accepted their confinement, unlike David who wanted out of this place. He just didn't know how to do it.

Over the next few weeks David tried to drive out of the place, again and again. He even tried taking the dirt road at the back of the motel rooms. Still the results were the same,. Without turning around he ended back where he had started from. Finally he gave up trying and tried to accept what was happening. It was harder than he expected but slowly he began to change, realising that he had a readymade family here and that was more than he had outside.

The women settled into the situation well but the children found the life boring even though David tried to keep them entertained. They would have to adjust to the situation as the adults had, but he wanted to make it easier for them.

Even though they didn't like the idea of being in a zoo, they had no real choice. Much as they would have been happier if it had been lush woodland, for the most part they accepted their fate and got on with life.

LOVE AND ITS CONSEQUENCES

Nicolas Massu

This story happens on a fresh morning of an autumn day. Roberto was a lonely pussy cat. He knew something was missing and felt he needed some company. Wandering around the countryside Roberto found a donkey named Revolver to be his friend. Revolver and Roberto got along pretty well; they would eat breakfast and play games together. Things were going well though one day they both felt pretty bored. Roberto did not think having Revolver for company was enough and he became desperate to find a female pussy cat. Having had so much trouble even finding Revolver the thought of finding a mate was very difficult for Roberto. Roberto and Revolver got to know the forest pretty well and all the animals in the forest. Finally Roberto knew what he really wanted was to kiss a female pussy cat. Sadly all of the domestic cats that Roberto knew about were on a farm owned by Joe. Joe was a terrible man who used to treat all of the animals in a bad way. So Roberto and Revolver knew they needed a way to get into the farm without getting caught. All of the animals in the farm were used by Farmer Joe in a bad manner. He forced them all into hard labour until they collapsed. There was not a single day that those poor animals were not forced into labour. The only two animals that were not treated this way were kept inside Joe's house. They were the female pussy cat named Daisy, and the dog named Bulldozer.

It happened that Roberto felt something from the first time he had ever seen Daisy and knew his greatest challenge was getting to see her, then make a way out of the farm without any problems. Roberto and Revolver watched the farm day by day and how Joe used to treat the animals. They watched the horse Daniel, who was the strongest and most agile of all the farmers' prisoners.

One day Daniel was left alone, mindlessly digging with a plough. Then it happened. Mastering his shyness Roberto took Revolver and approached the fence to talk to Daniel. Daniel said that the animals were digging a hole to escape but someone from the outside must finish it so Joe was not alerted. The animals in the farm were pretty desperate. Roberto and Revolver were the ones that would be able to rescue the animals, and make it so Farmer Joe could not keep treating them so poorly.

"In the stable where the hay is kept is a hole. The other animals have been digging it for week. They put hay over the hole to cover it, Joe doesn't know a thing. You should come back on Saturday and see for yourselves what the animals have done," said Daniel. "You need to do it without Joe noticing," he warned. "Otherwise he'll take you for himself and you'll be put to hard labour."

It was clear to Roberto that this was a carefully thought out plan and that the animals on the farm needed his help. Roberto and Revolver knew what they needed to do.

On Wednesday night Daniel went to the barn to break the news of their outside help to the animals. The animals thought it was a good idea but they didn't understand the real reason for Roberto's help. Roberto wanted to rescue Daisy to kiss her otherwise there was no benefit for him to rescue the animals on the farm. The animals decided they wanted to leave the farm and be happy. Daniel told them that Revolver and Roberto were coming on Saturday night to inspect the whole situation and see how this escape must be done.

On Saturday night Roberto with Revolver's help began to dig the hole to get into the farm. They had a problem. As they were digging the hole Joe came out to inspect an odd noise and all the animals suddenly got quiet.

Joe thought this was odd but went inside the house to go to sleep, saying, "Must have been a false alarm, stupid beasts."

Once Roberto and Revolver had dug the hole and got in, all the animals in the farm piped in chorus, "Thank you so much for rescuing us."

Roberto halted their gratitude abruptly, making them understand that they also needed to rescue Daisy from the house. The other animals became scared. Their saviour was only motivated by lust and they knew about Bulldozer - he was a Border Collie, who would do just as Farmer Joe commanded.

Roberto and Revolver spoke with the animals in the farm. "How are we going to get out of the farm with Daisy and without Joe knowing it?"

The animals had an idea that if they fasted every day then Joe would have to check on them and see why they would not eat.

Then the roosters said, "If we make noise in the middle of the night then Joe will have to get up and see what's going on."

The pigs thought this a stupid idea and suggested leaving the whole farm in such a mess that Joe would have to clean up, giving the animals a chance to escape.

Many of the animals and birds were giving their opinions as to how they would want to escape until Roberto silenced them again. "We will rescue Daisy or no one will escape," all the time knowing that all he wanted was to kiss her.

Revolver decided to bait Farmer Joe into a chase from outside the farm next Saturday night, then Daniel and the four cows could escape through the open gate. Daisy would still be locked inside so Roberto would get to the house through the hole. Once Roberto was in, the smaller animals and birds could go through the hole, Revolver would sound the alarm so Joe came out with Bulldozer to see what was happening. The plan was finalised and all the animals knew what they were going to do.

Every night the animals continued digging the hole, now with the hope that they could escape. Each day before the rooster crowed the animals would cover the hole with hay. Meanwhile Revolver and Roberto were watching what the animals were doing. They noticed that Daniel and the other horses were put into hard labour and were very tired; it was clear they had had enough of Farmer Joe.

On that Saturday night all the animals were ready to escape, waiting impatiently for the signal to get Farmer Joe out of the house. Roberto easily got inside the stable through the hole the animals had dug. Then Revolver made a noise at the gate. Farmer Joe came with Bulldozer out of the house; Roberto managed to get inside just before Joe closed the door. A great cacophony began, as all animals great and small, roosters and hens, ducks, pigs, geese and mice, turkeys and many other animals escaped through the hole. Joe noticed that all of the other animals except Daniel had gone but knew that horse had no escape once he closed the gate.

Daniel got angry and yelled at Bulldozer, "You idiot dog, don't you want to escape?"

Reluctantly Bulldozer replied, "Yes," eyes downcast as the dog's loyalty was broken.

"Bite him now!" Daniel bellowed, and Joe screamed as the Border Collie's teeth pierced the soft flesh behind his right calf. Bulldozer and Daniel fled through the open gate.

Daniel and the four cows went out, but Daniel remembered his promise to Roberto to free the two cats. Galloping up to the house, Daniel knew he could not knock down the front door. The hard labour had taken its toll on him.

Roberto looked at Daniel and yelled, "Leave us, escape while you can, fool, we'll be fine," before returning to kissing Daisy.

Joe was furious when he got back into the house that all his animals had escaped. Joe saw Roberto and Daisy and consumed with rage he killed both cats, saving them for later to eat. All the animals mourned the loss of both cats. For Revolver though, his only friend had been taken from him and grief had been subsumed by a need for vengeance.

Daniel went with Revolver and kicked Joe so hard that his back cracked and he was left for dead. Revolver entered the house and took Daisy and Roberto outside the farm to lie at rest together. Roberto would be remembered by all the animals as a hero and Revolver was comforted with the final thought that at least his friend finally found the companionship he was seeking, before the first scoops of soil were placed upon their joint grave.

MURDUROUS AFFAIR

Deborah L. McGrath

Angel was unhappy and lonely in her marriage, especially when her husband Tony went away on business trips all the time. It even made it harder for her having no family in Sydney. Tony had two brothers, Wayne and Kevin. Sometimes when Angel was in town, she would meet up with Wayne and have a coffee or a bite to eat with him. She looked forward to these days, but as the months went by her attraction for Wayne grew stronger.

One Thursday on meeting up with Wayne for coffee she asked, "Would you like to come over for dinner tomorrow night? Tony is going away again on a business trip."

With the slightest glint in his eye, Wayne replied, "Yes, that'd be nice. What time?"

Angel's heart fluttered. "About seven."

“That sounds nice,” said Wayne.

Over breakfast the next day Angel was thinking about Wayne when suddenly Tony interrupted her fantasy. “Did you hear me?” he asked.

“No, sorry,” replied Angel, annoyed to be interrupted. “What did you say?”

“Can you take me to the airport?”

“Yes,” Angel said, slipping back into her daydreams of Wayne.

After dropping Tony off at the airport Angel went home and had a long hot bath using an array of essential oils to relax and soften her skin. After her bath Angel put on her little black dress, knowing she looked great in it.

Ding dong, the front doorbell rang and before answering it Angel took one last look in the mirror.

“Hello,” she purred, “come in.”

As Wayne came in he kissed Angel on the cheek. Angel showed him into the lounge room and asked, “Would you like a drink?”

“Yes thanks,” replied Wayne. “I’ll have a Scotch and coke.”

As Angel handed Wayne his drink the accidental caress of her fingertips sent mutual electricity coursing through their bodies, unnoticed except for the breath suddenly caught in Angel’s breast. Turning her face quickly to hide the flush rising to her cheeks, Angel excused herself and went into the kitchen to prepare the oysters. When she returned with them Wayne joined her at the table.

“I Hope you like oysters?” Angel asked coyly.

“Yes thanks,” replied Wayne, thinking he might be in for a good night after all, and hoping Angel’s mind was on the same track.

After they had finished their oysters Angel went over to collect the dishes and went into the Kitchen to serve the main meal. She placed the quail in front of Wayne, excusing herself as she reached over him, her body gently rubbing against his arm. Before she sat down she asked, “Would you like some wine?” her lips subtly turned up knowingly.

“Yes thanks, that would be nice,” replied Wayne, his tone as cheeky as her smile.

Angel went over to the bar and poured two glasses of Pinot Noir, its ruby red matching her lipstick, before returning to the table and her meal. Wayne watched Angel working the small bird in her long slender fingers, moving a drumstick to her lips, the crispy brown skin in sharp contrast to the scarlet lipstick she was wearing. She consumed that meat with such abandon and pleasure, he could see it as they locked eyes. She slowly withdrew the bone from her mouth, sucked clean…

Wayne slowly moved his leg under the table, caressing her calf, sending chills down her spine. Wayne and Angel couldn’t hide their desire for one another any longer, and dragging Wayne to her marital bed they spent the night, gripped in throes of passion and debauchery.

The affair was begun.

“Hi Honey, I’m home,” Tony called out.

"Oh shit! He's home early. Get dressed and get out. I'll see you tomorrow at the same place," Angel whispered frantically.

She slid out of bed, putting on her dressing gown and going through the door. Instilling as much fake calm into her voice as she could, Angel called out, "Hello darling, you're home early."

"Yes, I finished my business in Perth and thought I'd catch an earlier plane home." Tony's attention was caught by a rustling sound, suggesting movement upstairs. "What's that?" he asked.

"It's probably just the cat," replied Angel, "but I'll just go up, and check."

Angel climbed the stairs, went into the bedroom and saw Wayne trying to climb out of the window. "What are you doing? You are making enough noise to wake the dead, are you trying to get caught?" she whispered.

"I'm trying to get out," murmured Wayne, his panic making him gruff.

"Honey, would you like a drink?" Tony yelled up the stairs.

"Yes, I'd like a Scotch and coke. How about we have it outside, on the patio," Angel yelled back.

As Tony went and made the drinks, Angel took Wayne quietly down the stairs and out the front door. As she went out to join Tony, he asked, "Who was at the front door?"

"It was the cat, she wanted to go outside," Angel replied, hoping Tony would buy the lie.

The next day Angel met Wayne at their usual place.

"Hello, darling" said Wayne, the excitement in is voice unmasked as he bent down and kissed Angel. The kiss was long and lascivious, promising more to come. Reluctantly breaking the kiss, Angel walked across to order coffee. The café was rustic, dark, with chestnut chairs and tables throughout. People followed in and out, the noise of their passing adding to an air already filled with small talk, the whooshing of freshly steamed milk and the rich scent of darkly roasted coffee. Upon her return Angel noticed Wayne looking at her as she swayed her hips back and forward tantalisingly.

"Have you come up with a plan on how we can…" She paused, searching for the right word. "…get rid of Tony?"

"We could poison him?" Wayne mused.

"How do you plan on doing it?" Angel asked.

"You know, my brother is a vet, and they use Lethabarb to put down sick animals. They only use what they need for the size of the animal and throw the rest in the bin. So I thought, I could get some from the Hazmat Bin and no one will notice," Wayne whispered.

"That sounds all right," replied Angel hesitantly.

"You don't sound happy with that," said Wayne.

"Yes, but will it be quick?" Angel asked, the catch in her voice unmistakable.

"Yes… well, it depends on how much you use, you know? Plus I'll check it on the internet, using the computers here," replied Wayne.

"Okay then," said Angel.

That night over dinner with her husband Angel was thinking about the conversation she had had with Wayne earlier that day. Suddenly a smile came to her face.

"What are you thinking about to make you smile like that?" asked Tony.

"Nothing much," Angel deadpanned. "Have you finished?" she asked, quickly diverting Tony's attention before he asked more questions.

"Yes thanks," replied Tony. "I have got to go back to the office for a while."

"Okay," replied Angel, clearly disinterested, "but I'll probably be in bed when you get home."

"Okay, I'll try not to wake you when I get back," Tony said.

Getting up from the table he went over and gave Angel a kiss on the cheek.

Tony didn't really have to go back to the office; instead he was going to the travel agent to book a holiday away for him and Angel. He hoped that by going back to Fiji where they had had their honeymoon it would reignite the passion and bring them closer again.

After Tony left, Angel rang Wayne. "Hi sweetheart," she seductively purred.

"Hi darling, what's up?" asked Wayne.

"Just wanted to hear your voice, and say I'm missing you," Angel replied with mock sadness.

"I'm missing you too, but hang in there. It won't be long now," replied Wayne.

"Okay then," Angel said, the sadness in her voice now real.

"How about we meet on Monday at the usual place?" Wayne asked excitedly.

"That sounds good," replied Angel, teasing him. "I'll see you then, but before you go I just wanted to let you know I'm alone and thinking of you."

After hanging up, Angel went into the kitchen and made herself a hot chocolate, taking it upstairs to the bedroom, and got ready for bed.

Monday came and Angel was looking forward to seeing Wayne again.

As she walked into the café she saw Wayne sitting by the window and thought how handsome he was, with his muscular physique, wavy blond hair and blue eyes.

"Hello, darling," Angel said with joy in her voice. She bent down to kiss Wayne while running a hand softly up his thigh, sending chills through him.

"Hi sweetheart," replied Wayne, thinking how lovely it was to be with her again.

The usual small talk carried them through until the drinks arrived. While sipping coffee Angel asked in a whisper, "What's our plan?"

"I'll probably call in and see Kevin on Wednesday, and meet you again on Friday," Wayne whispered.

“That all sounds good,” replied Angel, “…and that will have to be our last meeting for at least a month or two.”

Wayne’s face dropped; he couldn’t bear not seeing Angel for that long. “At least we can talk on the phone” he said apprehensively.

“No.” There was no room for negotiation with the tone she used. “You know, just in case anything goes wrong,” she said, trying to temper the disappointment in her own voice.

“Okay,” said Wayne, knowing that not seeing Angel for that long would kill him. They enjoyed the time they had left, but both of them knew that time was fleeting and soon they must part. The parting kiss was prolonged and deep.

The next day Wayne went over to see his brother. “Hi bro, how’s things?” he asked.

“Good thanks,” replied Kevin. “What are you doing here?”

“I thought we could go out and have a bite to eat?” Wayne said.

“Yeah, that’d be good,” replied Kevin, “but I’ve just got a patient to see first, then we can go.”

While Kevin went and saw his patient Wayne went into the back room to get some Lethabarb from the Hazmat Bin.

As Kevin came out of his room he asked, “Where do you want to go for lunch?”

“How about the Fraser?” suggested Wayne.

“That sounds great, it’s been ages since I’ve been there,” replied Kevin.

Slowly the days went by and at last Friday morning arrived. Over their morning coffee Tony asked, “What are you doing today?”

“Nothing much,” replied Angel, dreaming about the last time she and Wayne were together.

Tony got up from the table and kissed Angel goodbye and left for work. Angel cleared the breakfast dishes from the table and put them in the dishwasher. As she went up the stairs she was thinking what to wear as she wanted to look good for Wayne. She chose her low-necked red dress, knowing this showed off her beasts nicely. Angel took a last look in the mirror, adjusting herself for the best view.

At the cafe Wayne was sitting at their usual table. As she walked over to him, Angel noticed he wore his usual lustful smirk, clearly remembering the last time she had worn that dress. She snickered to herself, watching him fidget at having an involuntary rush of blood.

“Hi sweetheart,” Wayne said.

“Hi darling,” replied Angel, further teasing him by kissing the air by his cheek.

Wayne got up and pulled the chair away from the table for Angel and as she sat down he gave her a kiss on the lips.

Angel asked in a low voice, “Did you get some Lethabarb?”

“Yes. When are we planning to do this?”

"You know it's going to be Tony's birthday next Saturday and we will all get together for dinner, so I thought it could happen then," she said.

"That's a bit cold blooded, isn't it?" said Wayne, though after thinking for a brief moment, he added, "We can put it in his favourite whiskey, then drink a toast to his health."

"Who's the coldblooded one now?" Angel replied with a glint of more than just lust in her eyes. With everything now planned, Angel and Wayne enjoyed their final minutes together, knowing this would be the last time they would be alone. Their parting kiss was long and their hands continued to linger on one another, both afraid of letting go.

Angel arranged caterers to come in on Saturday, so she could enjoy herself with the family. Just before they arrived she went over to the bar and got down Tony's Glenfiddich, pouring in the Lethabarb unseen. As she was putting the bottle back Tony walked in.

"What are you doing with my best whiskey?" he asked.

"Just checking that you have enough for tonight," she replied.

"Do I have enough?"

"Yes," Angel said.

Ding dong went the front door. Phew! Saved by the bell, Angel thought. It was the caterers and she took them into the kitchen where they began to prepare the evening meal.

"Darling?" Tony called out.

“In the kitchen,” replied Angel.

As Tony came into the kitchen he said, “I have to go out for a while, I’ll be back soon.” Moving close, he kissed Angel on the cheek.

“Okay,” she said.

After he’d left, Angel went upstairs to have a long hot bath. While soaking in the bath she thought of Wayne and the life they would have together.

Tony walked into the travel agent and went over to Anne’s desk.

“Hi, do you have the tickets?” he asked.

“Yes, right here.” Anne handed them to Tony. “I hope you have a great holiday.”

“We will,” Tony said with a grin. As he drove home, Tony thought about the last time he and Angel were in Fiji and how happy they were then. He hoped that by taking this trip back to Fiji they would bring the spark back into their marriage and their bed. Arriving home, Tony went upstairs and walked into the bedroom. He could see Angel dressing in the bathroom. Quickly he walked over to his bedside table and hid the tickets inside the book he was reading. Seeing Angel walking in, Tony went over to her.

“Hi honey,” he said before moving in close to her right ear to whisper breathlessly, “I love that dress on you, remember what happened the night you first wore it?” His breath tickled the fine hairs on her neck.

“Yes, I do remember,” replied Angel. She clearly remembered the last time she had worn it, but instead of

Tony being there, she was with Wayne. As Angel was coming down the stairs the front door bell rang again. Upon opening the door she saw Wayne standing there and her heart missed a beat.

"Hello," she said, kissing Wayne on the cheek as he came in.

Returning her kiss, Wayne wished he could take her in his arms and give her a long passionate kiss, but he knew where he was and what was planned for this evening. Taking Wayne into the lounge room Angel announced his arrival.

"Hi Bro, happy birthday for today," said Wayne as he shook hands with Tony.

"Thanks," replied Tony. "Would you like a drink?"

"Yes thanks. I'll have a rum and coke."

The doorbell went again. "I'll get it," said Angel, "that'll be Kevin and his girlfriend Anne at the door."

Angel let Kevin and Anne in and showed them into the lounge room.

"Hi Bro, happy birthday for today," said Kevin, as he shook hands with Tony. Anne kissed Tony on the cheek, handing him his present.

"Thanks," replied Tony. "Would you like a drink?"

"Yes thanks," said Kevin. "I'll have rum and coke. Anne, what would you like?"

"I'll have a glass of wine thanks," replied Anne.

They were all sitting around and having a nice chat when the waiter came in and said, "Dinner is served."

"Thank you," replied Angel.

Showing them to the dining room, Tony went around the table and asked everyone what they would like, red or white wine. Conversation flowed nicely though dinner and everyone was enjoying the meal that was prepared for them.

With the meal finished the waiter carried the birthday cake in and everyone sang Happy Birthday to Tony.

"Thank you," said Tony. "Having you all around here has made it a great evening. Does anyone what a piece of cake?"

Everyone declined as they were all full from the nice dinner they had had.

"You can take some home with you," said Angel. "Let's go into the lounge room and have a cognac with our coffee. Kevin can you pour out the drinks please?"

Kevin went over to the bar to pour out brandy for everyone except Tony. He got down the Glenfiddich and poured some into a glass, then handed the drinks around while Angel passed coffee to each guest. The rest of the night went smoothly and time quickly got away from them.

"It's 11:30," said Anne. "We should be making a move soon."

"Yes," replied Kevin, "I'll just finish this drink."

Angel went into the kitchen to make sure it was clean and Tony followed her.

"Thanks for the great night," he said.

"Glad you had a good time," Angel replied.

After seeing their guests out and bidding them a safe journey home, they went upstairs and got ready for bed.

The next morning Angel awoke to find Tony still asleep. "Tony wake up, you are going to be late for golf," she said as she shook him.

"Okay," mumbled Tony, still half asleep. As Tony got up and went into the bathroom he felt groggy and thought a shower might make him feel better.

"Honey, can you make me a coffee please?" he yelled from the bathroom.

"Okay," replied Angel.

Angel went down to the kitchen and made Tony his coffee. As Tony came into the kitchen Angel handed his coffee to him. "Thanks, honey," Tony said. "I sure hope this will help me as I'm not feeling too bright this morning."

"It's probably from all the drinks you had last night," replied Angel. "Once you get out on the golf course you'll feel better."

"I hope so," he said.

He kissed Angel on the cheek and grabbed his golf clubs from near the front door.

Later that afternoon the front doorbell rang. Angel went to answer it to find two policemen there.

“Hello, Mrs Jones, I’m Officer Adams and this is Officer Banks. Can we come in, please?” asked Officer Adams.

Angel showed them into the lounge room.

“I’m sorry to inform you that your husband was in a traffic accident and died at the scene,” said Officer Adams.

“No! He can’t be!” cried Angel, tears welling in her eyes as she sat down on the lounge chair.

“Is there anyone we can call for you?” asked Officer Banks.

“I’ll have to call his brothers, Kevin and Wayne,” replied Angel.

“That’s all right, we can get an officer to call on them for you,” said Officer Adams. “We will stay with you until they arrive.” Officer Banks rang the station to arrange two more policemen to go and see Tony’s brothers.

Kevin and Wayne arrived together at Tony’s house and rang the front doorbell. Officer Adams went to answer the door and took the two men into the lounge room. Kevin and Wayne went over and gave Angel a hug.

“We can’t believe he’s gone,” said Kevin.

“Yes, it’s hard to believe he’s dead,” wailed Angel.

“What happened?” asked Kevin.

“We believe he fell asleep behind the wheel, this caused him to lose control and the vehicle went over a cliff,” replied Officer Adams. “But there will be an enquiry into the accident.”

“How long will that take?” asked Wayne, hoping it wouldn’t take too long so he could be with Angel soon.

“We’re not too sure.” Checking to see that Angel was settled, Officer Adams continued, “If there isn’t anything else we can do for you we will be on our way.”

“No, we’re as settled as we can be,” said Kevin, “but thanks for all your help.”

Kevin showed the two officers out, and thanked them again.

While Kevin was showing the officers out Wayne went over to Angel and whispered, “I’m missing you.” Hot breath caressed her neck as he nibbled the base of her earlobe.

Before Angel could answer him Kevin came back into the room. Seeing the look on Kevin’s face, Wayne blustered, “Just trying to comfort Angel.” He abruptly broke off his embrace, awkwardly trying to hide their involvement.

“Would anyone like a drink?” asked Kevin. “I know I would.”

“I’ll have a scotch thanks,” said Wayne.

“I’ll have one too,” Angel added.

Kevin went over the bar and got them all a scotch. They all sat there in silence for a while, taking in what had just happened.

“Would you like me to stay the night?” asked Kevin. “I can ring Anne and see if she can come over too.”

“Yes, that’d be great, I don’t think I would like to be on my own tonight,” replied Angel. Truly she would have liked Wayne to stay the night with her.

Kevin rang Anne and told her what had happened.

"I'll be straight over," she said.

The next morning Angel rang Tony's boss Matt, and told him what had happened.

"I'm sorry to hear about Tony." Matt's response was wooden, clearly unsure of what he was meant to say. "If there is anything I can do, please don't hesitate to give me a call."

"Thanks."

Angel was on the phone when Anne and Kevin walked into the kitchen.

"Who was that?" asked Kevin.

"It was Matt, Tony's boss. I was just informing him about Tony's passing. Help yourself to some coffee and I'll get breakfast ready for us all."

"Don't go to much trouble," replied Anne, "We can just have some toast."

While Angel was getting breakfast ready the front door bell rang.

"I'll get it," Kevin called. Kevin went and answered the door.

"Hi Bro, just come to check on Angel," said Wayne.

Kevin and Wayne walked into the kitchen in silence.

"Would you like a cuppa?" asked Anne.

“Yes thanks,” replied Wayne, glad to fall into any conversation.

They all came and sat around the kitchen table to have their breakfast.

“Did Tony ever talk to you about what he would want, if anything happened to him?” asked Kevin.

“He wanted to be cremated,” replied Angel, “and his ashes scattered over the ocean.”

“We can go together tomorrow and make enquiries for his funeral if you like. Then everything will be prepared once the police release his body,” Kevin said.

“That’d be good, one less stress to worry me. Thanks,” Angel mumbled, her despondency unmistakable.

When they all left that morning, Angel went into the lounge room and walked over to the bar and got down the bottle of Glenfiddich. She poured the remaining liquid down the sink. Putting the bottle into a plastic bag, she took it outside and smashed it, then put it in the rubbish bin, knowing that tomorrow was garbage day.

Two weeks after Tony’s death the front door bell went and Angel found two well-dressed men at the door.

“Good afternoon, Mrs Jones, my name is Detective Blake and this is Detective Russell. May we come in please?” asked Detective Blake.

“Yes,” replied Angel, showing them into the lounge room.

"We would like to ask some questions in regard to your husband's death." Detective Blake was to the point and broached the issue without hesitation.

"Yes, that would be fine," replied Angel, taken aback by the forwardness of the detective.

"As you know we had to do an autopsy on Tony. The blood results have come back showing that he had Lethabarb in his system at the time of his death."

"Sorry, Detective, you'll have to explain. What is Lethabarb?" Angel hoped the look on her face was confusion and not guilt.

"Lethabarb is a drug that is used to put animals down when they are seriously ill," replied Detective Russell.

"That sounds awful," said Angel. "How would that have gotten into Tony's body?"

"It could have been put into his drink, or his food," replied Detective Blake. "We are asking everyone that was at the dinner that night to have a blood test. We want to know if Tony was the only one drugged or the only one who had been affected." It was clearly not a request. "Do you still have the empty bottles of wine from that night?"

"Yes, they're in the recycling bin," said Angel. "What about the other bottles we used that night?"

"Yes, we have to take them too."

Angel went over to the bar and took out the bottle of rum and the bottle of brandy. Detective Russell excused himself as he went outside to the recycling bin and collected the empty bottles. Upon returning he had a glass in his hand. "Was this glass used on the night?" he asked.

"Yes," replied Angel, "Tony was drinking his Glenfiddich out of it, and when I was tidying up that night, I noticed that it was chipped so I put it in the bin."

"Okay," Detective Russell said, his tone giving nothing of his thoughts away. He collected the full bottles offered by Angel, adding them to a bag with all the empty bottles and the chipped glass.

"I think we have everything we need…for now," said Detective Blake.

Angel showed them to the front door, her movements mechanical.

"Thanks for all your assistance," said Detective Blake. "We'll be in touch if we find anything." "Thank you, Detective Blake" said Angel as she slowly closed the door on the detectives and used its handle to steady herself and her racing heart.

A week after questioning Angel, Tony's body was released. She rang Smith and Sons Funerals, and made arrangements for Tony's funeral to be held on Monday. At his funeral there were people from his work, plus family and friends paying their respects to Tony. Angel was putting on a brave face though the occasional tear slipped through the stoic mask. It wasn't hard pretending that she was sad and missing him. Not even someone from the academy would have seen through her performance that day.

A week after Tony's funeral, Detective Blake and Detective Russell returned to Angel's house,

"Sorry to call on you so soon after your husband's funeral, but we would like to ask you some more questions about the night leading up to your husband's death." Again Detective Blake's tone left no doubt that it wasn't an option to refuse.

"Okay, please come in," replied Angel and showed them into the lounge room.

"We found Lethabarb in Tony's glass," said Detective Blake, "...but not in any of the wine or any of the other bottles we took away. Each of the blood tests for the other guests have all come back negative." Not giving the chance for interruption, Detective Blake continued, "What was the relationship like between Tony and his brother Kevin?"

Angel assumed the line of questioning was due to Kevin being a vet and it would have been easy for him to get Lethabarb.

"It was good," she said, though paused as if apprehensive. "But, they had a big fight about a week before his birthday."

"Do you know what this argument was about?" asked Detective Russell.

"No, sorry, you'd have to ask Kevin about that."

"Will do," Detective Blake mused. "Who was making the drinks that evening?"

"Tony made the first lot of drinks, he poured the wine at dinner, and Kevin got the drinks after the evening meal."

"Do you think Kevin could have put the Lethabarb into his drink then?" asked Detective Blake.

"He could have," replied Angel, "but I wasn't watching him, and I don't think he'd have done that to his own brother."

"Okay." Detective Blake was clearly still sceptical. "Thanks for your help today."

Angel showed the detectives to the front door, bidding them a good day.

Not long after the detectives left, Angel rang Kevin.

"Hi Angel, how are you feeling? What can I do for you?" he asked.

"The detectives were here and they were saying that Tony was poisoned with something from a veterinary clinic. It was found in the glass that he was drinking his Scotch from."

"How would Lethabarb get into his glass?" asked Kevin.

"Well, you were the only one that poured the drinks out after the meal. Why don't you tell me?"

"What are you saying?" Kevin asked, outraged. "That I killed Tony?"

"Well you are the only vet here," replied Angel.

"I'm telling you now, and I'll only be saying it the once." Kevin said each word slowly and deliberately, trying to drum the meaning into her. "I did not kill Tony."

"Okay," said Angel, her disbelief unmasked.

"I'm sorry, I've… I've got to go" said Kevin. "'Bye for now."

"'Bye," Angel mimicked. When Angel hung up she was happy with herself. If anything happened she was coved by the call to Kevin and her implications.

The next day the two detectives went to Kevin's practice.

"What can I help you with?" Kevin asked.

"As you know we are looking into your brother's death. We would like to ask you some questions if you can make the time," Detective Blake said. "Is there somewhere we can go and have a talk?"

"Yes, the clinic is quiet today, we can talk in my office." Kevin led the way.

"Did you know that Tony was poisoned with Lethabarb?" asked Detective Blake.

"Yes, Angel rang me yesterday and told me. I've administered it often enough, what an awful way to die," replied Kevin.

"Yes, it is," said Detective Blake. "I believe you had a fight with him a week before he died. Can you please tell us what it was about?"

"It was about money. I asked Tony for a loan because the practice isn't doing too well."

"And?" Detective Russell prompted.

"Isn't it obvious? He said no."

"How did you feel about that?" asked Detective Russell.

“I wasn’t happy about it,” Kevin said hotly. “The practice is my life, and it would’ve been nothing for him to give me that money.”

“So, tell me more about what happens when you get angry.” said Detective Blake.

“I didn’t kill Tony if that’s what you are asking,” replied Kevin angrily.

“Well you had the opportunity,” said Detective Russell. “You have access to Lethabarb here in the practice.”

“I‘m a vet, what d‘you think I use to put animals down, a fuckin‘ gun?”

“Okay,” replied Detective Russell.“Just calm down a bit.”

“I’m plenty calm thanks…” Kevin said, reining in his temper. “My brother’s just been killed and considering you’re the second person to accuse me of killing Tony, I think I’m being really calm…”

“Who’s accused you of Tony’s death?” asked Detective Blake.

“You and Angel,” replied Kevin.

“We are looking into your brother’s death, we need to question everyone that was there on the night and follow up on any other avenues of inquiry that present.” Detective Blake looked towards his partner, prompting the next question.

“Why do you think Mrs Jones made that implication?” asked Detective Russell.

“When she rang she accused me, because I was the only one that poured out his Scotch that night.”

“Well she is right, by all accounts you were the only one pouring out the drinks after the evening meal,” said Detective Blake. “It doesn’t look good for you.”

“I loved my brother.” Kevin’s anger was swiftly being replaced by sadness and his eyes welled with tears. “I wouldn’t even think to hurt or kill him.”

“Will you give us access to the clinic so we can we have a look at the room where you dispose of the Lethabarb when you’re finished with it?” asked Detective Blake.

Kevin took the two detectives into the back storage room. The detectives split up, asking Kevin to stay outside as they took a good look around the room.

“Is this room ever locked?” asked Detective Russell.

“It’s only locked when the practice is closed,” replied Kevin. “So anyone could’ve come in and taken some Lethabarb.”

“That’s enough to lose you your license, but right now I’m more interested in if you are accusing someone else?”

“No. I’m just saying that anyone could’ve come in.”

“Thank you, Mr Jones,” said Detective Blake. “There is nothing else we need to ask or see for now.”

Kevin showed them to the front of the practice. Everything about him seemed to exude defeat

After the detectives left Kevin rang Wayne.

Wayne could tell from his tone that something was wrong. “Hey bro, what’s up?”

“I’ve had the detectives here questioning me about Tony’s death,” replied Kevin angrily.

“Yes, they’ve been here too. They said he died from Lethabarb which was in the glass he drank from…” Letting his sentence die off said more than any words Wayne could find.

“Yes, that’s what they said to me as well.” Kevin’s anger flared again at the further implication of Wayne’s silence.

“You sound angry about that,” said Wayne.

“Yes I am. They are accusing me of his death.”

“Why are they accusing you?” Wayne tried to sound incredulous though even he knew it sounded fake.

“You know damn well I use Lethabarb here to put down sick animals. Plus I was the one that poured out the drinks after the evening meal.”

“Oh,” said Wayne. “When you say it like that, it almost sounds like a confession, but you know that they have to question everyone.”

“Yes, but you didn’t see the way that they were questioning me, like I was guilty of killing Tony.”

“Well I know you wouldn’t kill your own brother.” Wayne bit down at the irony of him uttering those words.

“Thanks, bro,” said Kevin. “It makes me feel a bit better that you believe in me.”

“Well hang in there, and I’ll give you a ring later on during the week.”

When Wayne hung up he wanted to ring Angel, because he was excited that their plan was working so well. It had been so long and he was missing more than just her voice. Though he knew better than to call now, it was still too risky.

Three weeks later the detectives were back at Kevin’s practice.

“He’s with a patient at the moment,” said the receptionist.

“We’ll wait,” said Detective Blake and they took a seat in the empty waiting room.

When Kevin come out the two detectives waited for him to say goodbye to his patient before Detective Blake announced, “Mr Jones, we are arresting you for the murder of Tony Jones.” Detective Russell moved behind him as he drew out a pair of handcuffs.

“I didn’t kill my brother,” said Kevin, but it didn’t make any difference. He was restrained before he’d uttered the final word of his protest.

As Detective Russell was putting on the handcuffs he read Kevin his rights. “You are not obliged to say or do anything unless you wish to do so, but whatever you say or do may be used in evidence. Do you understand?”

“Yes but I didn’t kill my brother!” he yelled as he was escorted from his office.

Two days later Anne and a lawyer came and saw Kevin in jail.

“Hi, sweetheart, this is Mr White our lawyer to help you with the case,” said Anne.

“Thanks, darling.” Kevin stood and moved to shake hands, his wrist catching on the restraints anchoring him to the table. “Hello, Mr White, thank you for taking on my case. How does it look?”

“It doesn’t look good,” replied Mr White, “and please call me Jason.”

“What do you mean, it doesn’t look good, Jason?” The embarrassment of the handcuffs was quickly forgotten.

“You had motive. In the police report it said you had a fight with your brother a week before his death while asking him for a loan. Also you got very angry when you were questioned by the police.”

“Yes,” replied Kevin, “but what do you expect when they were accusing me of Tony’s death? And yes I wasn’t happy with Tony’s decision but that’s not enough to kill him.”

“But then there is the opportunity,” said Jason. “You being a vet makes it easy for you to get Lethabarb.”

“I know it isn’t looking good, but I loved my brother and I didn’t kill him,” insisted Kevin.

“Okay then. Hang in there and I’ll get to work on it.”

“Thanks again, Jason” said Kevin.

“I’ll see you soon.” Anne leaned in to kiss his cheek. “I love you,” she whispered.

"I love you too." Kevin stifled a sob.

Outside the jail Anne asked Jason, "What do you think?"

"It doesn't look to good for him," replied Jason. "There's a lot of evidence against him, but I will look at the police report again and go and see his brother Wayne, and Tony's wife Angel about that night. Also I'll need to talk to you some more as well."

At last the jury had made a decision. It had been six long months for Kevin, but at last he would know if the jury had found him guilty or not guilty for his brother's death. While he sat there waiting for the judge to come out, he thought about the months he had spent in jail and about the court hearings he had to sit through. Looking over at the jury he tried to predict the verdict that would change his life for better or worse, but no one was giving anything away. They might not find him innocent, because it felt like sometimes the prosecution was twisting the questions and his answers around to suit their case. The lawyer was good and it was hard for him to make out that Kevin had killed his brother. The one thing that surprised him was Angel's testimony, saying he could've poisoned her husband because he poured out the drinks that night after the main meal and also because as a vet he had access to Lethabarb. This upset Kevin very much and it was as if everyone was conspiring to take his life from him. The hardest thing for Kevin about being in jail was the loneliness and not been able to hold Anne in his arms. She visited him as much as she could though the gaps between visits seemed to be getting longer and longer.

"Please all stand for the Honourable Judge Davies," called the clerk.

Kevin prayed the jury would find him not guilty, because he couldn't bear to be in prison for much longer.

"Please all be seated," the clerk said after Judge Davies had assumed his position.

Indicating the accused, Judge Davies said, though it sounded as a holy commandment to Kevin's ears, "Please stand."

Turning to the jury the judge asked, "Have you reached a verdict?"

"Yes Your Honour," replied the head juror. "In the matter of Kevin Jones versus the Crown, we the jury find the accused Kevin Jones… guilty." The head juror said each word calmly and clearly as though the outcome meant nothing.

Kevin couldn't believe what he heard and near fainted as he fell into the chair.

"Kevin Jones, a jury of your peers has found you guilty of the murder of Tony Jones. I sentence you to 25 years in prison with a non-parole period of no less than 10 years."

The judge had passed the verdict and then motioned to the bailiff, "Please take the prisoner away."

"I didn't kill my brother!" yelled Kevin, tears streaming down his face as he was dragged away.

The next day Jason and Anne went and saw Kevin.

"Darling, you know that they have it wrong," said Anne. "You're innocent. I know you couldn't have killed Tony."

No matter the mask she wore Kevin could see the strain the trial had placed on her.

"Thanks, sweetheart," replied Kevin. "I couldn't believe that they found me guilty."

"Don't worry, we will appeal against the verdict," said Jason.

"Yes, please do," said Kevin.

Two months later Wayne and Angel were boarding a plane to Fiji using the tickets that Tony had bought months ago. Sitting back comfortably in their seats the plane took off.

Wayne turned to Angel and asked, "Happy?" He gave her a passionate kiss, his taste lingering on her tongue.

"Very," she sighed.

Though the means of achieving it were atrocious, their affair ended happily ever after.

NANNA'S GIRL

Linda Dearlove

A head full of curls
coloured ginger 'n' spice
Twinkling eyes
could be naughty or nice
Mischievous giggle
that infects all who hear
Can't help but smile
whenever you're near

A mountain of energy
coiled tight like a spring
With a coating of laughter
ready to burst from within
Pure innocence portrayed
although not always true
How could a nanna
not be captured by you

The smile on your face
can light any room
You radiate a love
that can chase away gloom
Chubby cheeks, button nose
Such a kissable face
You're just the right size
for me to embrace

You've no idea
of the comfort you bring
The cuddles you give
can make my heart sing
photos and memories
I have them all stored
With you in my life
I could never be bored

SHE HATED HIM

Arri R. Taieb

Judge Donovan looked at her with sympathy and sadness. "The court finds you innocent, Mrs Butler. You're free to go and I hope you have the energy and fortitude to overcome this terrible tragedy that has befallen you," he said quietly. "I hope in time you will be able to pick up the pieces and eventually be able to live a full life again in spite of your husband's tragic death."

"Thank you, Your Honour," she answered with a shadow of a smile and he returned the smile with great kindness.

She hated him! She hated him with a passion. She hated him with every bone in her body. Even though he was dead, she ***still*** hated him. Why on earth had she married him? He had been an abuser, a liar, a cheat and a rapist. She had been seven months pregnant when he had forced himself upon her for perhaps the hundredth time, brutally and without any regard for her comfort or wellbeing. Three hours later her beautiful little baby girl had been stillborn. The doctor had quizzed her but ***he*** had stood there with her and answered for her, "No, she's been perfectly okay, doc, she just caught her foot in the sheet as she got out of bed and fell really heavily on her stomach across the footboard which just happens to be solid oak." The doctor had glanced at her with a look that begged contradiction but she had been weak, too frightened to fight back, knowing if she did the beating that would follow may just be the final beating ever.

He was also the most narcissistic person she had ever known. He wanted people to like him, to love him, to think him smart and funny. He bathed in their adulation and at parties and gatherings he was like a king holding court and if he wasn't the star around which all the little satellites revolved, she would be on the end of his fist when they returned home. Nobody would have believed her, they all thought him kind and charming; extremely attentive and loving to his wife - always his arm around her waist, smiling at her, offering her the olive from his drink or a canapé from a passing waiter.

However, there was one thing she had learned. If she asked him for something within reason, in front of a group of people he would accede to her wishes purely to show how magnanimous he was before his adoring acolytes. So she had asked him for a fishpond for her birthday and he had laughed and told her she was a funny little thing and he didn't deserve her and how low maintenance she was and then kissed her in front of his adoring fans. The fishpond had been installed but not just any fishpond; this was a Koi Carp fishpond, a "Look how ***I*** take care of ***my*** wife" fishpond. The fact that it was ***her*** fishpond held no interest for him; it was all hers to look after and only occasionally would his strolls through the garden take him anywhere near it.

She had been incredibly careful, making sure she stayed on his good side - not stepping out of line - which meant not having an original thought of her own, cleaning his laundry, preparing his meals on time; in fact being the good little wifey he expected her to be. In return, he only smacked her two or three times a week, telling her how lucky she was to have ***him*** as her husband and not some bullying kind of monster. Slowly she built up a business friendship with the guy at her local pet and exotic fish store and was soon using his contacts to import her own exotic fish. At last, at long, long last she made her move. She was terrified and excited all at the same time.

"I think someone has stolen all the Koi" she whispered, dreading his reaction because of course it would undoubtedly be her fault that they were missing. "Either that or a heron has been fishing for them".

"What? You're mad, you don't know what you're talking about" he rasped, grabbing her by the scruff of the neck and pushing her violently out the door. "If anything's happened to them, I'll beat your frickin' head in. They cost a frickin' bomb." He dragged her through the garden by her hair until they reached the pond where he promptly threw her to the ground. Gazing at the water he didn't see any sign of life, not a single ripple broke the surface. He peered closer, thinking he could see a vague shape in the shadow of the weeds and suddenly he was falling, pushed violently with a strength she didn't know she possessed. He plunged headlong into the water, which instantly began to boil around him as hundreds of flashing mouths and tails and fins of the piranha went about their deadly work. It didn't take long and when the police arrived following her frantic phone call, all they had been able to rescue was a perfectly clean skeleton still wearing his clothes and the solid gold identity bracelet and necklace. 'A terrible tragedy' the judge had called it and the insurance company had not been able to argue with that, ultimately paying out a figure that would keep her in the lap of luxury for the rest of her life.

"No," she thought as she sat sipping her pińa colada on the terrace of the villa with the Spanish sun toasting her body a rich espresso coffee colour, "the terrible tragedy is that I'm having to enjoy this all by myself, but I'll soon change that and next time will be totally different and it will be on my terms. I've learned my lesson well."

SIEGE OF SAINT AUGUSTINE

Matthew Nicholson

David Kavanagh, usually the strong, stoic picture of the hard man, sat in the courtyard and wept. A moment, seemingly unending yet happening in but the single beat of a drum. The tears streamed from his blue eyes, normally so icy cold, now melted by sorrow this day. David could not lift his head, for his stare was fixed firmly upon that which he hugged so tightly in his arms: Jennifer.

She was a slight girl; eyes brighter than the emperor's own jade, a depthless green; hair, as dark as sails at midnight, cascaded down her face, oddly reminiscent of David's very own. Her lips so full used to remind him of the vermillion coats of the royal guard, but the lifeblood which had promised such sensuality as she came to age now ran through David's fingers.

The cobblestoned streets of the Saint Augustine Chapel ran red this evening; the mixture of blood, sweat and tears only further diluted by the heavy cold rain that had set in earlier today. A day that until the setting of the sun had been no different from any other on this desolate, isolated rock. However with the darkening atmosphere, on an already dreary day the pirates of Westermince had attacked. The monks of Saint Augustine had grown lax during this prolonged period of peace, and had not noticed the darker grey of rising smoke against the cloudy sky, a sky that had hung over them as a low ceiling all day.

That was until they heard the resounding clamour and cacophonous roar coming from the town below. The first villagers had reached the walls of the chapel seconds before the cannon fire erupted in the crowded streets below. The pirates, so well prepared for the raid, had brought along field artillery. Even from the top of the bluff where the chapel sat, the monks could see people being flung bodily into the sky by the ten pound balls.

David, as Abbot of Saint Augustine, led the defence of the chapel and had held open the heavy, iron banded wooden gates for as long as he dared. As the seconds turned to minutes he started to become frantic as his youngest sister Jennifer had not yet arrived. She had been living in the care of friends of the family in town since the passing of both parents during the previous war eight years ago. David rarely saw Jennifer due to his obligations to the church, though he loved her dearly. She was the only light brighter than God in his life, and her being seemed to light the path for so many of that town.

David had no choice left, he could not leave the chapel open any longer and leave exposed those who relied upon him for protection. David ordered the gates closed. As the intricate mechanism which controlled the gates was driven to life, age-old gears squealing as metal grated against metal, then he saw her. Jennifer had reached the top of the hill and was running as fast as she could to reach Saint Augustine, like its namesake the salvation of Cragenmore's people. Behind her, however, came the horde of pirates that had caused such destruction below.

The mismatch of colours - red and white striped shirts, leather breeches weatherworn and splattered with mud or worse, and other odd flashes of vibrant colour from the most flamboyant amongst them - added further visual disorientation to the already overwhelming auditory chaos that approached.

Leading the band was the infamous Westermince captain, Billy McDoogal. His red and black knee- length coat, thrown back by the increasing strength of the storm, displayed his bare chest, as scarred from battle as rumour held. Rumours that suggested the man was a daemon and could be killed by no mortal means. A rumour that David had difficulty in dismissing viewing that flayed flesh. The flickering of firelight set off lightning flashes across his brass buttons and golden teeth. The glint in Billy's eye was missed by none as he levelled the long rifle, Redemption as it was known amongst his crew, squarely at Jennifer's back.

David pleaded with the girl to hurry, his normally deep voice hoarse with fear and the certainty of his loss.

"Come on, Jenny, you're almost here, the gates won't stay open much longer!"

The passage into salvation grew tighter with each beat of his frantic heart. David knew though that he could not reverse the order. Throwing open the gates now for his little sister would mean the death of them all. These pirates were not the type to parlay, and prisoners were just more mouths to feed.

David, standing in the aperture between the rapidly closing gates, reached out for Jennifer, a miniscule three feet from life, when the clap of Redemption beat her to the walls. Jennifer faltered in her stride, the force of the round between her shoulder blades throwing her into David's waiting arms. He was just able to pull her into the courtyard as the gates slammed shut; and though the final clang of the gates' brace being lowered into place signalled the beginning of the pirates' siege on Saint Augustine, it signified naught but the end for David's beloved Jennifer.

Though he wept, David knew now was the time for pragmatism. He used that sorrow to forge his resolve, and his anger to hone it like the razor-sharp blade he had not drawn for years. For though Saint Augustine had enjoyed peace for many years the monks of that chapel had not abandoned their rigorous martial training. For it was they who protected the world from absolute madness, kept the tools of this world's destruction from the hands of evil, and protected that which was most fragile, faith in the human heart.

Like the monks' training, Saint Augustine was kept remote for a reason; it was the storehouse of all of the Royal Families' most powerful and obscure artefacts. The great sword of Kaziclarz, its ruby blade slaked by the blood of three hundred virgins sacrificed to its deamon lord; the shroud of Mezzastein, said to drive all who view it into a bloodlust driven frenzy; the Maelstroms Glove, a seemingly innocuous black glove, easily overlooked in any wardrobe, which could unleash furious bolts of electricity to incinerate one's enemy. These were but a few of the horrific items kept within the deepest vaults of Saint Augustine; and now it fell upon David's shoulders to keep these items safe

David left the courtyard and began the ascent into his quarters. David's piety was without equal and though his station warranted reward, he lived in the same manner as his initiates. The austere grey bricks of his room welcomed him, the single iron sprung bed the only piece of furniture. The only decorations to be seen were the Star and Moon emblem, the sign of Jeremiah the Pure, to which his nightly prayers were sent; and the sacred alter which held his no-dachi, the sword responsible for ending the last war, Kinslayer.

David picked up Kinslayer, that familiar weight, the cold smoothness of the ebony sheath against his fingers. Finally he examined the slip knot tethering the blade to the sheath. David had tied this knot in the hope of never needing to draw the sword again, but with the knowledge that should the blade be drawn, it would taste the blood of many men before being returned to slumber.

Though he knew the guilt of taking life again would haunt him David drew on his resolve and knew it was time to act. He returned to the courtyard of Saint Augustine, rallying any who could hold a sword in Jeremiah's honour behind him, setting what meagre defence could be mustered in this time of crisis.

The gates to the courtyard shuddered against the repeated cannon shot. Pirates howled in anticipation, just waiting for the breach, so their fun may begin. The only sound louder than the staccato black powder blasts was that of Billy McDoogal's laughter. Revelling in the chaos he had brought Billy urged his crew to greater heights of action.

"C'mon ye' dogs we haven't got all night; tear those gates away with your fuckin' hands if ye' have to. Any man I see not working to get me into Saint Augustine, the most holiest of holes, will be given absolution, for I hold in my hands Redemption!"

The bombardment of the chapel's gates persisted for hours, and David could see the youngest amongst them being worn down by the unending cacophony of shouts, screams and cannon fire. David ordered these… boys… inside the chapel with the elderly, women and children, tasking them with protecting the soul of Cragenmore village but knowing that if the pirates breached their line, any survivors would wish they were dead.

As the doors to the inner chapel closed the first splinters appeared in the stout outer gates. With each ensuing volley more and more wood was blasted away until the gap was large enough for a man to get through. Then the cannon fire stopped.

David was tense, expecting the assault, but knew that with such a small opening the chapel would be easily defended. Though their numbers were small they were the elite force in this confrontation. Years of training had brought them all to the point of almost superhuman martial prowess.

David however had not taken into consideration that pirates by their very nature do not fight fair and would not assault as an honourable enemy would. This oversight lasted only as long as it took for the muzzle of one of the field pieces to enter the breach in the gate. That black glossy barrel promised death to all inside and before any could take cover, it spewed forth a canister of shrapnel.

Thin pieces of metal twisted by the concussive force of the cannon tore into the courtyard. The peppering spray ripped and maimed all in its wake before embedding itself in the main walls of the chapel. No level of training could have prepared the monks for what they had faced. Once again Billy had brought chaos to this town. A monk may defend against the sloppy sword strokes of four untrained men, but against the assault on all sides from numerous, inanimate steel, they had no chance.

Every man in that courtyard had been downed and no matter how heavy the rain fell that night, their blood ran faster and stained those age-worn cobbles like no time in the temple's history.

Meeting no resistance, Billy walked into the courtyard and approached David, his crew at his back.

"Well, Father, it seems that the powers that be are with me this day. I want to thank ye for protecting the valuable treasures, oft talked of round these parts. They'll be a fine addition to me collection."

Billy turned to the crewmates behind him.

"Well, lads, bein' a church an' all we'd better pay the proper respects, don't ye think?"

The singular chorus that arose from all of his crew showed their devotion to the captain.

"Aye!"

Billy started his recital and let his gaze meet with that of the twisted flesh that was David, Abbot of Saint Augustine.

"Thy will be done, unto kingdom come, in the name of the Holy Father let me bestow upon ye, me final blessing."

Throughout this recital Billy moved the end of Redemption to David's breast, the sharp retort of the rifle punctuating the end of the blessing and signalling the end of the assault of Saint Augustine. Walking towards the inner chapel Billy cried out a final word to his crew that evening.

"Let's get them doors open, lads, our fun this evening has just begun and within this temple lies the key to my release. I think I can even smell the bonny lass from here… AHAHAHAHAHAHAHA."

THE PINNACLES

Linda Dearlove

My mouth was dry. Drier than I ever remember it being before. The surface of my tongue felt and tasted like it had been covered in a thick layer of dirt. Swallowing was almost impossible and only served to remind me of how parched my mouth was.

In whichever direction I looked there was a barrenness, a desolation of the earth, interspersed with great mounds of peculiar and irregular explosions of rock formations. It struck me how similar to my own situation the landscape was. My mind vacuous and unforgiving, only interrupted by thoughts so contorted and aberrant as though, like the rocks, a giant hand had scattered them and left them where they fell. With no meaning or order as to their placement.

Dirt! Surrounded by it! Tasting it, feeling it. The grains of sand, like my thoughts, burrowing their way into every part of my body and irritating me. The roughness of the rocks reminded me of the harshness of my reality. No love. No caring. Nothing to soften the grittiness of life. Even amongst the rocks, where one would expect to find shelter and relief, there was none because the rocks were like sandpaper against my skin.

There was a silence that seemed to stretch forever, enveloping me and overwhelming me with a sense of isolation. Yet if I listened carefully, straining my hearing to its limits, there could be discerned echoes of arguments past. Sounds that haunted my mind and were only amplified by the complete absence of sound surrounding me. No one to hear my heart-wrenching cries for help, my impassioned pleading, for someone, anyone, to listen, to care. To stem the incessant flow of blood that was seeping from within.

My heart was haemorrhaging, shattering into tiny pieces, innumerable as the grains of sand on which I was standing. Gradually weakening with each feeble attempt to keep my body functioning. But it was fighting against the weariness, the utter abandonment of hope that had become the very air that I was breathing. So that with every exhalation, the desire to survive dissipated into the dry and desolate place that I found myself in.

The last drops of moisture left within me were gathering in the corners of my eyes. Yet not enough could be found to cause it to flow over the edge of my eyelid, like a dam bursting, releasing its life-giving liquid in a gush. Then slowly trickling away, creating its own course down my face. Leaving behind streaks of skin, washed clean by my tears. But there was no energy left within me to search inside and muster up enough moisture to let the tears form fully, so there was no spilling over, no starting their healing path down my scorched and weathered face.

My mind was drawn back from its wanderings to my surroundings, the strings of thought trying to gather together as one and focus on the changes that had occurred around me. However it now seemed to be moving as if in slow motion, tiring quickly under the constant barrage of my insidious thoughts. It was as though my mind had been overrun by a dust storm, making it even harder to focus. My thoughts were being tossed and blown in every direction and I was unable to control where they went at all.

Suddenly I became aware that night had fallen and all that I had been able to peruse earlier had vanished from sight, only to be replaced by a blackness. A blackness so complete that it was as if some unknown event had stolen my eyesight. Searching desperately for even the tiniest pinpoint of light, yet finding none. There was nothing, nothing but the blackness. The darkness seemed to grow, not only around me but inside me, as if it had invaded my very being. I succumbed to the absence of light and let go. No more strength left within me to fight against being sucked into the blackness, drowning in the midst of it. Yet amid the letting go there came a peace, a relaxation. Something felt lighter, like the layers of dirt, the aridness of my environment just disappeared. I became aware of snippets, tiny strands of memory scattered within my mind, where I had experienced this peace and relaxation before. However they were so minute and so random that the darkness quickly and quietly obliterated them as soon as they arose. Soon there was nothing, nothing but the blackness. A black hole, devoid of any sound. The blood that had been leaking from my fractured heart was complete and the shattered fragments were dispersed in every direction like the grains of sand that I was sinking into.

The darkness was now unfathomable, and there was nothing else.

NOTHING...

THE WARBLING

Arri R. Taieb

She looked absolutely beautiful - perfect in fact, as she turned away from him with a smile on her face and the most feminine wave of her oh! so exquisite alabaster hand. As she led him across the concourse his mind was so far down in the gutter, he wondered whether he would actually have a clean thought ever again. He chuckled to himself. If the women were all like this, well maybe he wouldn't mind his enforced posting to this god-forsaken hole of a planet after all. It was the furthermost planet in their system and the previous ambassador had been stupid enough to suffer a fatal accident whilst out hunting, shooting himself in the foot and not getting proper medical attention until far too late and had died a slow and agonising gangrenous death.

The Interplanetary High Commission had told him, in fact had promised him that the posting would only be for three months and he had made sure to get that contract signed by the Commissioner himself before he agreed to it.

His escort invited him to be seated beside her in the sleek black limousine as it pulled away from the spaceport with a purr and headed off through the streets of the city. As they sped along, she pointed out all the usual tourist sights, some familiar because of the holocards he had seen back on his home planet and some so completely alien to him they were totally beyond his comprehension. Luckily, the Ambassadors' Mansion was on the southern outskirts of the city, the high-end of sophisticated living, while to the north was the filth and squalor of the mines and minerals, which they were plundering for their own home planet. The indigenous inhabitants of this planet were so far behind in the evolution chain the Commission had been able to just walk in and take what they wanted.

"Tonight there is a banquet in honour of your arrival," she said. "Also performances from some of our most famous artistes in the land. All are eager to meet you and make you welcome. Until tonight then, Ambassador." She smiled as the limousine deposited him on the steps of the mansion and with a wave of that alabaster hand was gone.

Servants appeared as if by magic and escorted him inside the beautiful building, pink marble with shimmering gold accents all plundered from the planets' mines. His new aide-de-camp and head of security led him to the boardroom, showing him his office and his secretary's connecting office, through the lounge to various other offices and meeting rooms and at last to his private apartments where he was left to enjoy a long leisurely soak in a pink marble sunken bath. After dressing in the long flowing robes - which had miraculously appeared laid out for him across his huge circular bed, cool and pleasantly scented with smoky bark overtones and cinnamon - he descended from his apartment to the next floor to a gallery overlooking the main entrance foyer, where he could watch the arriving officials and artistes. He saw her arrive and went down a long curving staircase with ornately carved balustrade to meet her.

She introduced him to the local dignitaries and he came to realise after several limp handshakes and half-disguised insults on his part that the inhabitants of this planet would do anything to please. He became more insulting and eventually found he was enjoying himself immensely. The banquet began and he feasted like a pig, all the while throwing great quantities of the local fermented rubbish that passed as alcohol down his throat. Then came the entertainment. He'd never seen anything like it in his life! He was thrilled. The last act was the most enchanting. Tiny elf-like creatures no higher than his hip with fairy-like wings trilled clear notes and the air around him resonated with a multitude of vibrating colours. Each colour that passed him, he could smell a different scent of fruit or perfume of a flower. He was in thrall to these little creatures. He turned to his escort.

"I must have one," he whispered to her. The smile dropped from her face as though she had been whipped.

"But Ambassador, they're Warblings."

"I don't care what they are, I want one, get me one," he growled.

"Yes, Ambassador, of course, Sir."

Much later when all the guests had left, she found him on the balcony gazing at the star-spangled sky. "Mr Ambassador Sir, may I ask, Sir? Do you know <u>anything</u> about the Warblings, Sir?"

"Yeah, they sing like angels and have wings of gossamer, right?" he slurred.

He could barely hear her as she whispered to him, "Mr Ambassador Sir, a Warbling is a very special being; they only ever bond with one owner, Sir. Nothing can or ever will break that bond - except death."

"So much the better then, at last a being that can be faithful. Never in my life did I think I would ever come across such a phenomenon - always thought it was a myth," and with that he groped his drunken way to his apartments and flinging himself across the bed he promptly passed out.

When morning came, he rolled out of bed feeling like a million dollars with no ill effects from the previous evening's excesses. He arrived at his offices and made his presence felt in no uncertain terms. He felt good ordering his staff about, they were totally compliant and eager to please and because of this, he became more insulting and abusive than he ordinarily would be. Just before leaving his offices for the day, he delighted in kicking his Chief of Staff down the stairs simply for glancing at him while he was picking his nose. He'd never felt so good!

He retired to his apartments early and decided to play with his Warbling before dinner. She sang and danced for him, she loved him; he was her owner and meant the world to her but he was feeling so high on adrenalin that he couldn't wait to indulge himself and did so unashamedly. This became the pattern of his days and while the little Warbling became more subdued with his ill-treatment of her, he just looked forward to returning to his home planet after three months of debauchery on this very welcoming world.

At long last the day arrived and he packed his bags, settled back in his limousine and was whisked to the spaceport where his ship took off without delay. "Home," he thought delightedly whilst he stroked his bags stuffed full with priceless ill-gotten gains that he'd stolen from the mansion. He didn't give another thought to his staff who had looked after him and served him faithfully or to the little Warbling to whom he had handed a death sentence. He hadn't understood nor even cared when he was told that Warblings will only ever bond with one owner and now she sat on the grassy rise outside the Ambassadors' Mansion, tears sliding down her little elfin face, watching the pinpoint of light that was his ship dwindle away into the night sky. Her owner had gone, her love had gone; there was nothing left to live for. Slowly she curled her tiny self up and faded away.

THE WEIGHT OF LEADERSHIP

Matthew Nicholson

Jacob took the last few steps toward the locked metal door, his pace slowed by the still weeping wound in the top of his right thigh. Each step of his heavy military boots clanged resoundingly on the warship's grated flooring and echoed down the tight corridor. Though his steps were slow, his heart raced. With trepidation Jacob reached out with his right hand, the slight tremor irrepressible as he placed it upon the solid metal latch. "I'm in the Navy," he thought, "how can my hands shake just opening a simple door?" Trying to bolster his courage with thoughts of the years of training he had completed was useless, not because he was poorly trained but because as a Chief Warrant Officer he knew this was no ordinary door. The latch thudded across, metal on metal groaning in protest; to Jacob though it was as if the ship herself warned him away.

Throwing open the door, an aperture of blackest pitch welcomed him. Before walking in Jacob could already feel the sensory deprivation kicking in, though slowly his ears became attuned to an unusual sound from within. It was like a slowly leaking tap; drip, drip… drip. The sound of the drips however were unlike water. Where water made a clear splash as it hits metal, this liquid burst as it hit the floor, as if it were heavy, thick. Mustering his courage Jacob drew his sidearm, it was a Glock .45, and the heavy familiar weight calmed him, giving a sense of peace. Bravely, he stepped forward into the gloom, making but two steps before his nerve began to waver. It wasn't the blackness but the stench that stopped him in his tracks; it was strong, sickly sweet and metallic, seeming to cloy the air about him as a miasmatic fog. Jacob instinctively knew what the stench was and fortifying himself, he moved deeper into the void. It only took one more step before his feet began to stick to the floor, every movement slowed, as he trudged through the unseen muck as if wading through the foulest of swamps. As the sludge coating the floor got thicker Jacob noted how the drips had now increased in number and were steadily getting closer. He continued to cautiously move forward until one of the drops hit the back of his neck, freezing him instantly. A shiver coursed through him, icy fingers running down his spine, two fold; initially because he knew what had just dripped down upon him, and then in the way the lukewarm fluid slowly trickled along his skin, feeling like it tumbled over itself, cooling and congealing.

Jacob could not take the darkness any longer, though he feared the knowledge that would come with light. At the moment, every other sense screamed at and horrified him further; the heady scent, claggy floor and the sinister downpour from above. He needed to see, for better or worse and thought, "At least if the bastard is still here the Light'll startle him!" Reaching into his vest Jacob removed the last flare left; all the others had been spent, trying to signal for help to the US satellites in orbit. A vain hope. No help had come and it had been months now. Running his fingers along the smooth surface of the barely visible orange tube to find the flares ignition cap, Jacob wondered, the irony not lost on him, "I can pop this final flare and kill him to save myself and starve to death in the next week; or save it for one last chance at salvation." An almost inaudible squelching like the cautious stalking steps of a bloodied predator made up his mind in half a heartbeat. Closing his eyes to shield them against the initial ignition, Jacob popped the cap with his thumb, holding the flare high as he raised his gun and dropped to a defensive stance. Even through lidded eyes there was a harsh red glow from the flare, a pinpoint of radiant white where the magnesium burnt brightly… and short lived. There was an uncertain time limit that Jacob was consciously aware of; he had anywhere from fifteen to twenty five minutes of burn time until the darkness descended upon him again, though with his .45, once he had sight of the… monster, only seconds and bullets would be needed.

Though the racing in mind made it feel like minutes, forcing ever more adrenaline into his blood due to his perceived need for action, only the initial three seconds of ignition had passed. Hoping to find the killer still dazed by the sudden light, Jacob slowly eased open his eyes, letting them adjust to the new brilliance. It only took until the smallest part of the room had come into focus before Jacob's eyes widened in horror. The space was one of the smaller storerooms of the USS Indefatigable, a recommissioned destroyer from the early 2000s. The room was meant to be a four metre square box with steel grated flooring, wall-mounted storage racks and two centralised freestanding shelves; it had access doors on both sides, the one Jacob had entered through and another, standing ajar. Though the opposing door suggested that He had fled, Jacob did not register the sound of retreating footsteps. Whether they were there or not would later be a source of insecurity, however within his present Jacob could comprehend nothing further than the transformation of the storeroom. While consumed in darkness his imagination had run wild, showing him all manner of unspeakable horrors; experiencing the sticky floor, thick toxic smell and blood rain; but now he was caught in a scene more daemonic than what he imagined to see in the deepest circles of hell. It was a gore room.

The horizontal shelves had been pulled from the wall leaving nothing but the jutting metal supports which had then been ground down to jagged wall spikes. Most of the spikes had nothing more than putrid rust-coloured stains, splattered across the sheet metal, evidence of acts so inhuman Jacob couldn't begin to imagine. Sweeping his eyes from left to right Jacob needed to imagine no longer; on the third spike of the right-hand wall his fellow crewmate, Caleb hung, the spike driven through the left side of his chest at an upward angle just below the sternum. The mangled hole was a mixture of ripped flesh, lacerated organs dripping a mixture of foul fluids, and worst of all, pink tinged white, shining out like opals in the flare's illumination, Caleb's smashed ribs. The uniform around his arms and legs had been torn away, wire wound tightly around his wrists and ankles running to anchors in the floor and ceiling, drawing him out suspended and spread eagled. The wires biting so deeply in his struggles that he had his blood coursing along them while his heart had still beaten. The wires were now coated in thickly congealed blood, making Caleb appear as a marionette, strung up by crimson cord. The culmination of this horror did not come until Jacob saw the look upon Caleb's face; his eyelids had been cut away, forcing him to watch as this… thing… had done this to him. A signature-like symbol, an inverted crucifix encircled by a serpent, was carved into his forehead;

though it was the hopelessness in his eyes that haunted Jacob most of all. As Jacob came to the point where he felt he could endure no more, a drip from the ceiling hit his neck again. Knowing only more horror was above, he looked up, as if compelled by Lucifer himself. There hung mesh bags of all different sizes. Smaller ones either held nothing but pulp or the severed limbs of Jacob's other crewmates, so mangled as to make the owners themselves unidentifiable. Larger, duffle bag sizes had what appeared to be whole corpses crushed in to fit, bones sticking out at odd angles where the men had been contorted in ways not meant for any healthy human. From each of the various bags, at least a dozen in number, steady drips of blood fell to the floor, the speed of the leaks showing the freshness of the kill. Finally, following that red precipitation, Jacob allowed his gaze to fall to the floor where more limbs were strewn about with abandon and in varying degrees of both decomposition and apparent ritualistic consumption. Skulls laid in the corner, piled up into a pyramid, an altar of sacrifice even the ancient Inca would have been proud of. Most of the skulls had been picked clean though a few still had flesh on them, gnawed and mangled, the thing seeming to eat specific parts first. All had ears removed and dark, empty eye sockets while the noses remained. Then the door slammed shut, the finality of that deep metallic boom sounding as a death knell to Jacob's over stimulated senses. He didn't look; terrified as he was Jacob had enough control to know where he stood and his orientation to the opposite door. Wrenching on the trigger he fired off all ten rounds blindly, turning towards his own exit as he did so. Forgetting all training in his flight for survival, Jacob ran, as quickly as his legs would carry him.

Jacob took random turns, left and right through the bowels of the ship; he didn't care if he got lost, at least he'd be alive. As he rounded a corner, his haste to escape made him careless. His right leg fatiguing from the wound delivered earlier that day had his foot drooping and it snagged on an upraised pipe, causing him to fall and crack his temple hard against a maintenance valve, now partially painted red in his blood. Jacob had just enough time before falling into blissful unconsciousness to register what he assumed to be his final thoughts. First was the grey, black blur moving in on his prone form and simply, "So this is how it all ends?" and then all was black.

World War III had broken out just over four years ago following acts of coordinated aggression against America by combined Chinese and North Korean forces. California was the first to fall, being occupied by Korean troops who swiftly and unexpectedly took control on Port Hueneme, the United States west coast home of naval activity. Newly developed submarines had gotten into the harbour unnoticed, sinking and disabling any war ready vessels before disgorging an occupation force capable of securing at first the main port and then moving into the state. The goal of this move was to secure a military stronghold upon American soil, placing an Asian incursion in a secure position to move out from and gain territory, state by state. The justification for subsuming California was because it provided the invasion force with an easily established supply line for munitions, food and further reinforcements via sea and air, and afforded the conservation of the rich American resources which could be drawn upon in any dire emergency. The subjugation of the state was easily completed by the initial force due to both the rapid and brutal nature of the incursion, and the synchronised Chinese diversion. China had directed this against the home of democracy, Washington DC.

The Chinese had provided two days prior warning for a holocaust-styled nuclear strike capable of decimating the entire country unless the United States agreed to be annexed by Communist forces and fall under immediate Chinese rule. Of course America would not be dictated to and controlled by the threats of terrorists. America had been expecting such an event to occur and had been preparing since the end of the Cold War. Raising their defences the US cast an air to ground intercept net wide in what seemed to be an impregnable yet invisible shield. For the next two days there was the usual bluster from politicians on both sides, and as can be expected when politicians talk, nothing happened; then the missiles had darkened the skies, a veritable murder of crows converging on a single point.

Where the initial threat had been for the flight of seven high yield nuclear warheads across the breadth of America, on the 27th of April what was now thought to be every hidden bunker across both China and North Korea opened each spewing forth innumerable high explosive yet non-nuclear missiles. Washington was the sole target, the aim to remove the head from the capitalist beast. Although the American defence system was strong it was also thinly spread to protect the suspected significant targets of the attacks. It did not take long for the smaller missiles to break through that net and begin the sustained bombardment. Three hours after the first breach, little of the city remained; worldwide news broadcasts showed the attack in real time, unable to hide the suspected hundreds of thousands of casualties… until the broadcasts themselves abruptly ended.

America quickly mounted a resistance, deploying both main and reservist forces to begin retaking their territory. The resistance numbers were also quickly bolstered by the rapid withdrawal of US forces from the Middle East. Fighting was fierce, both sides sustaining major losses and the costs both financial and in human life quickly adding up. The American troops had access to better equipment, however the relatively minimal reinforcements from Australia, New Zealand and the United Kingdom, all of whom were still caught up in Middle Eastern deployment, had them fighting severely outnumbered. In comparison the invasion force was a seemingly endless tide flowing in from Asia. The sheer volume of highly trained Chinese troops being committed to the front made any defence slow and laborious and showed years of planning and preparation for the assault.

After eight months of fighting the momentum of the invasion was halted, and though the loss of American soil had ceased the Allied forces were also unable to reclaim what was theirs. The Communist frontline, a veritable impenetrable wall, held the Allies at bay while consolidating the ground they had won. Although not the easy occupation expected, and seen early on in the incursion, the Chinese clearly had no intention of relinquishing their new territory without inflicting a huge cost to the West. Newly erected outposts supplying long range bombardment to the battlefront, the fortification of existing buildings into bunkers of hostility and the random grids of landmines and improvised explosive devices kept the cost in manpower alone inexorably high.

Throughout this period of conflict, America had been in hurried negotiation with Russia, knowing them to be the only country strong enough to supply the means of ending the budding World War. Though clearly reluctant to come to the aid of the Allies, eventually enough incentive was given by the American government for Vadim Pewten, the President of Russia, to come to their rescue. Riding in like a knight in shining armour Russian troops were rapidly deployed to the front. With a heavy reliance on artillery and their implacable tank battalions, the Russians alone were able to drive the Asian invasion back into the sea within a matter of months. Soon after came the mobilisation of the Russian Navy, Vadim Pewten intent on committing more man and firepower to the defence of this newly formed alliance. Then the retaliations upon Chinese and North Korean borders began, hostilities beginning with renewed ferocity.

This swift turnaround in the flow of battle quickly prompted the Asian ambassadors to enter into peace talks, now willing to risk subsumption by the now larger Allied forces. Again the politicians' waffled numerous talks and meetings were held, all without tangible outcomes; more constructive debates were seen in the kindergarten playground. After six more months of interminable political posturing a cessation of hostilities was agreed upon, the world tentatively returning to normal.

Regardless of the outcome of the negotiations, America had not wasted this time; conscription and been reinforced, the standing army growing with each passing day; decommissioned ships were refitted and brought to the ready; and any factory capable of manufacturing military resource was tasked to do so, from bandages and ammunition to ration packs and communication arrays. This was a country unified in its efforts for security. America's place as an ongoing global superpower had been tested; though their position was weakened they remained unbroken, resolving to regain their status of being the greatest country in the world, even if they had to do so through military superiority and unforgiving cultural suppression.

Throughout the consolidation of their powerbase America maintained its ties to the Allies until they felt strong enough to ensure that their position would not be challenged. When this day came there was the request for the immediate withdrawal of all foreign troops from American soil. The withdrawal progressed smoothly and troops returned home country after country until only the Russian forces remained.

Though repeatedly asked to remove their troops, each reiteration becoming ever more forceful, Vadim Pewten finally showed his true colours; he was really a black knight and his armour was far from shining. In hindsight all could now see how easily peace negotiations had gone. The success of the suppression was not because of the Allied threat towards China and North Korea but rather revealed to be part of a larger Communist plot.

All the initial invasion force had aimed for was to limit their own casualties while weakening the American position. The Communist coalition knew that the US was capable of repelling a smaller invasion, however with their forces deployed abroad with a large enough initial attack they would be forced to call upon unlikely allies in a time of crisis, thus allowing for an amicable occupation by the Russian force.

Once the Russians were in place World War 111 erupted. Due to the hurried preparations during the initial peace negotiations, America was already in a state of heightened readiness, quickly responding to the new threat and able to meet hostile forces head on. The conflict was brutal, being carried out on land, air and sea. Lives were lost at home and abroad, and though the flow of battle ebbed and flowed on a quickly deepening sea of blood, it continued unabated for a further nineteen months. Thus bringing us to the deployment of the Indefatigable and Jacob's dire predicament.

The USS Indefatigable had been deployed to the mid-Atlantic on an extended patrol assignment, tasked with monitoring, reporting and if capable, intercepting any movements made by the Russian fleet. Though she was an old ship, an Arleigh Burke class destroyer built in 1988, she was reliable and had been in constant service for twenty years. Her armament, though now antiquated was still formidable; ninety cell vertical missile launchers able to unleash the offensive tomahawk cruise missile as well as utilising a ballistic missile defence from the Aegis system. Cannon and lightweight guns ranged from 25mm to five inch shells adorned both fore and aft decks. Not the largest or fastest ship in the fleet, the Indefatigable was easily recommissioned, quickly deployable and more than capable of serving the purpose she was tasked with.

Shortly after taking up her assigned position, coordinates 31°25' north, 39°27' west, The Indefatigable caught sight of an unfamiliar vessel at the edge of their horizon. It was thought to be a Russian ship, however each time pursuit was instigated the vessel quickly retreated outside of the Indefatigable's patrol area. The game of cat and mouse was afoot and continued for weeks until the ship's senior officers were convinced that this was a diversionary tactic to draw away American eyes and allow for a greater fleet to pass unnoticed. Tiring of the game the Indefatigable commenced pursuit in earnest. Engines were put into the frantic pace required for interception, quickly bringing the old ship up to cruising speed and slowly closing the distance to their quarry. Once it was clear that the warship was committed to the pursuit the other vessel turned about, facing the Indefatigable head on rather than fleeing as had been its previous behaviour. As the distance between the two ships diminished the Russian opposition became clearer.

She was a small ship, no longer than sixty metres; sharp angles defined her hull painted in the uniform matte black of a typical stealth vehicle, the only point of colour the shocking scarlet of the hammer crossed sickle insignia. Doubt remained no longer, she was Russian, she was enemy. It was clearly a new ship for the commanders knew nothing of what they faced, had never even seen a ship of similar design before. As is the American way they felt that a good offence was always the best defence; long range missiles began to streak into the sky while two self-propelled torpedoes sped towards the unnamed ship, great white sharks closing in on a defenceless seal cub. Unexpectedly, the Russian ship responded quickly, moving forward and out to the starboard side of the Indefatigable, deftly avoiding both torpedo strikes while the black rain, missiles adjusting their trajectories, continued to descend unerringly on target. Fifty metres before their impact upon the Russian vessel the sky itself erupted, a cataclysmic inferno as unexpected as the first fireworks on the 4th of July. Every missile had been shot down, the whole barrage entirely ineffectual and the casual ease with which the Russians had defended themselves gave off naught but a sense of disinterested contempt.

Following clear, direct and open hostilities from the Indefatigable it was as if the Russian vessel had been given permission to strike; thus began its counter attack. The deck at the bow of the ship opened up on concertina hinges, seeming to fold back upon themselves as the wings of a great vulture; the folds of metal providing shielding and soon to be discovered support to the huge octagonal barrel that emerged. The 80cm bore of the bizarre weapon was dark as it was raised and secured into position; for such large and heavy machinery the whole movement was smoothly executed. Dread set into the leaders of the Indefatigable, this was clearly no prototype warship. Not long after the barrel had been secured, lights began to illuminate down each exterior face of the weapon, a pulsing red strobe that was seemingly absorbed by the surrounding black metal. Almost imperceptibly at first the cannon began to glow; dull orange transformed into a malevolent red finally turning into a blindingly brilliant white. Not wasting any time in the face of such an unknown force the Indefatigable had already made moves to set itself to evasive manoeuvres. The smaller ship then displayed its impressive agility, pivoting almost motionlessly in the water, tracking the older ship and keeping her well within the Russians' sights; then they fired.

The helm of the Indefatigable was there one minute and gone the next, for whatever the Russians had fired completely decimated the ship. From the single round, fires raged across the deck where munitions had instantly ignited still within their weapons from the heat of the charge. The remaining crew scrambled around the deck trying to prevent the spread of the fires while trying to form some method of countermeasure, confused commands being issued, each at odds with the previous. Then a second volley hammered into the Indefatigable, carving mid ship through storerooms and crew quarters. The battle was over before it had really begun. The Russian vessel showing supremacy in every way had demolished the old destroyer effortlessly. Stowing the strange weapon back within the hull, the small ship turned about ready to stalk her next prey. What remained of the Indefatigable was left disabled and helpless, without communications and a skeleton crew to waste away to nothingness in the Atlantic sea, thus elevating Jacob into his first position of command.

Jacob rushed up the aft stairs to what remained of the deck to survey the damage. He was horrified; whatever weapon had been brought to bear on the Indefatigable was nothing he had ever seen before, not even within the sci-fi films he loved to watch back stateside. Used to cleaning up the mess following a gun fight, Jacob expected to see bullet holes, bodies and blood painted around the decking. What he now faced was melted and charred metal, pools of steaming, unidentifiable liquids and anything still vaguely recognisable as a human casualty looked like meat left in a microwave for far too long, this sickening thought reinforced by the stench of burnt hair and seared flesh rising to his nostrils with each laboured breath. The horror of the scene settled over him, an image so vividly burnt into his mind he knew it would haunt his dreams for the rest of his life. Taking a deliberate step forward Jacob brought to the forefront of his focus all the leadership training he had undergone and took stock of the situation rationally. Spot fires continued to burn in several places along the length of the deck, the black smoke rising into the sky as solid columns from the oil that fuelled them. Looking for help from the crew that remained, Jacob was able to muster fifteen men, and splitting them into three squads he methodically set them to work quelling the fires lest they spread further, putting the survivors in an even more dismal situation. Jacob took control of the moment, organising the crew while worrying both about their current situation - if they could not stabilise what remained of the ship she would sink, leaving them all to freeze to death in the frigid waters below - and hoping that he was not the most senior officer left aboard as no training could prepare anyone for the complete shit storm they were currently in.

The smaller groups worked well, the hiss of powder extinguishers signalling that work had begun to put out the fires raging along the length of the deck; though numerous areas burned, once they had been starved of oxygen they were out no matter how much fuel remained available. It took four hours to get the fires under control, however to Jacob time passed instantaneously. The action was frenzied and the constant demands for his attention and guidance ground down any remaining mental reserves.

Night was just beginning to fall when he was finally satisfied that the ship would at least see another day. Calling the remains of the crew together, Jacob surveyed the situation. Things were far worse than he had thought. As a Chief Warrant Officer he held seniority over those that remained. Four apprentices from the kitchen huddled together wary of the three Petty Officers who were still barking orders at the dozen regular seamen. This was all the crew that remained. Skill-wise they were well short of what they needed to sail the Indefatigable, let alone make the running repairs needed for them to limp back to an American base. Food stores were low, however Jacob was thankful they had a plentiful supply of fresh drinking water. The communication array along with the evacuation boats had all been destroyed by the sweeping Russian shots. As far as Jacob could see they were all stuck on a floating grave, left helpless until they either ran out of food, were made easy prey to the next enemy ship or they all went mad; though for tonight he knew what was most important was to lift the morale of those that remained.

Calling for the kitchen hands, Jacob tasked them to make the best meal they could with what remained of both the storeroom and the kitchen supplies. Time passed quickly and once the meal was prepared Jacob called the whole crew together. They sat at an improvised long table on the main deck. Surveying the line of dishevelled men, covered in dirt, soot and worse, Jacob could not help but see the similarities between his current situation and every time he had seen images of The Last Supper. His crew huddled around him as lowly apostles and there was a terrible feeling in his stomach that this story would have a similar ending.

Rising to his feet Jacob addressed the crew. "Men we face hard times, no one here cannot see that. The ship is un-sailable, only through luck and the sheer willpower of we few have any survived. We must band together. We must work as one. We must be strong if we are to face this adversity. If we can do this then we'll make it home. God does not send the strongest of his warriors to face the greatest challenges, it is those challenges that make us great warriors!"

Looking around the assembled men, locking eyes with each in turn, Jacob knew he had their support. "You all worked well today, when it mattered most you met every challenge, and without those efforts we would've sunk outright. We will face another day, more yet unidentified challenges and many more hardships. They are challenges we will face tomorrow, for tonight we live, tonight we feast.

Our cooks have prepared this bounty in all of your honour; eat well for tomorrow the real work begins."

Resuming his seat, Jacob looked around at what were now his men, his responsibility; the strain of leadership had already begun to settle on him, heaviness about his shoulders, an unaccustomed weight. Though a shiver ran down his spine at the prospect of such responsibility he took heart as his eyes passed over each sailor; the ones he knew well, Matthew Finean, Caleb Hortega, Max Hughes, Carlos Sanchez and Shane Cormac. Then there were the acquaintances, the men Jacob knew by sight and by role but not by name, seven in all. There would be plenty of time over the next few, he hoped days but expected weeks, to get to know them better. That left the final five who Jacob knew nothing about. Moving to sit with the cluster of unknowns, he joined in their conversations, catching names here and there. They focused on the uncertainties of the situation, worries about friends and family back home, the possibility of the Russians returning to finish what they had started, the shortness of their food supply. Jacob settled them, allaying what fears he could and bolstering their spirits. The whole time though, he was aware of the man he had learned was Ray.

Ray was a small man, 5'2" and skinny, he couldn't have weighed more than 110lbs. Though clearly physically fit, a job requirement for any able seaman, he seemed sickly. The usual tan of a lifetime of sea spray, sunshine and windburn was more of a sallow yellow, as if his veins pumped puss rather than blood. Dark grey hair topped his head, so consistent in colour as not to be the greying of age yet neither was it the black of youth. Jacob could even see the curve of his scalp through it because it was so thin, adding more to his already skeletal and ghoulish appearance. His face was angular, almost hawkish, his prominent nose sharply hooked at the end. Everything about the man was unappealing but it was his eyes that bothered Jacob the most. Like his hair they were grey, a dull emotionless slate made darker by the heavy bags beneath them and the almost comical depth at which they were sunken. Worst of all they conveyed no hint as to what was going on behind them. It appeared as if he was unbothered by their circumstances, sitting calmly and quietly, eating his meal, not joining in on the conversations of the others and deadpanning any attempts Jacob made to engage him further. Ray gave Jacob the willies, and Jacob knew instinctively that he would need to watch him. Something was not right about Ray and how nonplussed he was in this situation, almost as if he expected to be here. These however were musings for another day, it was getting late and everyone needed what little rest they could get before the real work began. Jacob drew the attention of the remaining crew, setting up a rotating roster for night watch and dismissing the rest to their bunks. Being the last to go below decks to find his rest, Jacob paused, looking up into the clear night sky, and thought, “Now it begins, I just hope I can get us all though it.”

As Jacob had expected the days had turned to weeks. At regular intervals the crew had burnt off the magnesium flares they had been able to salvage from the ship’s remains. With each flare came the hope that it would be the signal which brought them salvation, the signal which was seen by one of the many passing American satellites. No help came; this caused the crew to worry for two reasons. Firstly for their own sakes and the dire situation they were in; food supplies were getting dangerously low, even with strict rations in place, and their limited success at fishing had had their ship stores running dangerously low since mid-last week. Secondly, if no help had come by now then things must be bad back stateside. The Indefatigable was one of the smaller ships, but there had to be something wrong if all the signal flares being burnt at regular intervals had not been noticed by America's worldwide famous sky high surveillance. Though both issues weighed heavily on Jacob, he was more concerned with how the crew were dealing with it. Such psychological strain could only last for so long, before a man, any man, broke. Jacob's worry was that the cracks had already begun to appear. Some of the men were becoming overly aggressive, the sheer number of fights that Jacob needed to break up was growing daily, and his time taken away from more important issues was increasingly shortening his own fuse. What was really grating on his nerves was that the fights were breaking out over the most ridiculous shit, the absurdity of it all was infuriating and Jacob was sure the next fight would be over the colour of an orange. Then there were the men that were already giving up. Jacob could see it in their eyes, they were waiting for death, an end he often felt like bestowing on them himself. The hopelessness within them was not only contagious but it made the men sloppy, stupid accidents happened frequently from mere inattention, often resulting in an injury which the crew as a whole could ill afford.

What worried Jacob most of all was how Ray continued to deal with the situation; he went about his work without complaint, doing what was needed though nothing more and continuing to maintain his distance from the rest of the crew. What Jacob found most disconcerting was the thin wry smile that seemed to be permanently painted upon Ray's face, as if he enjoyed being here. Did the fool not realise the seriousness of the situation? Or had he already lost it, so far gone within the madness that his body continued on mechanically, as if he ran on autopilot? There was nothing more Jacob could do though. At the moment Ray caused no trouble, there were so many greater issues within their present that to draw attention to what he believed was strange behaviour would only single himself out and draw into question his ability to lead those that remained. "I'll just keep watching him," Jacob thought. "I'll wait for him to slip up and once he steps out of line then I'll have reason to remove him." Through narrowed eyes Jacob observed Ray, none of his suspicions salved from watching the slow and deliberate movements Ray made while repairing an exposed pipeline. Breaking away his hawklike stare, Jacob looked up to the blue sky above. "At least the weather is with us and nothing overly bad has happened," Jacob guessed.

That night the storm hit. "Just, fuckin' typical!" Jacob yelled as a rogue wave toppled him in his rush to take up his position on the main deck. "This is what happens when you bless your good fortunes," he thought bitterly as he regained his footing and began taking in the conditions. It was rough; cloud, a mottled grey against a depthless black, blanketed the sky so thickly that neither moon nor starlight shone through. Wind blew from the west, sweeping the deck clear of any debris and jettisoning crucial supplies that were not secured properly. Jacob heard a clamour behind him, a rumbling that grew quickly; he was able to dive safely out of the way only moments before the unrestrained oil drum rolled through where he had been standing and launched itself down into the colourless pitch below. The sea roiled, throwing up freezing foam as waves twelve feet high battered the Indefatigable's side. Ensuring his position would not be threatened by any more unsecured resources, Jacob fully surveyed the situation;.With the ship disabled as she was there was no way to bring her about to face the waves, each thunderous hit reverberated along her side, each impact hitting the hull with the force of a wrecking ball. The Indefatigable faced the risk of either capsizing outright or being torn apart from the relentless battering. Waves continued to roll in and it was clear that nature was the greater force in this battle for the retort of water slamming into metal changed in pitch, the hull plates themselves giving in to the unending assault.

Though the situation as a whole was grim Jacob kept calm by focusing exclusively on the here and now. What was needed was a way to force the ship around so that the wave's impact could be absorbed along her full length. What was needed was a rudder, but lamentably that had been irreparably damaged during the Russian attack. Jacob called Caleb and Max over.

"We need to make a sea anchor to pull us around and we need it now!" Jacob hollered over the shrieking wind.

Caleb, level headed as always, responded quickly. "I'll get the men searching the crew quarters for any scraps of canvas we can…"

"Don't forget their duffels," Jacob hurriedly interrupted, "they'll add some extra drag. Get the men on it. I'll go collect the rope we'll need.".

With a plan in place Jacob became resolute, quickly issuing orders and dismissing the men to their work. Caleb and Max ran back into the bowels of the ship, rousing the remaining crew and setting them to action. While they were at work below Jacob ran around the main deck, careful to watch his footing, traversing the slippery and constantly shifting surface to gather up a length of rope long enough for the purpose.

The rope he found was eighty feet long, two inches thick and made of bright yellow nylon. It was harsh on both his eyes and hands and the rough synthetic fibres bit deeply as he coiled it in hands numbed by the frigid wind. Returning below decks he joined the crew, and casting his eyes over the mound of collected canvas bags he thought, "Is that all they could find?" A ball of hot lead settled into his stomach. There were only eighteen bags; it would have to be enough for they had no other option. Not having the time to worry if it would work or not he set the men to work, getting each bag tapered into a funnel and tied off to the main rope. The large mouths of the canvas funnels would each catch immense amounts of water and tapering down the restriction of flow would create drag upon the main line, hopefully enough to meet its intended purpose. As a sea anchor it was ugly and ungainly, taking three men to awkwardly wrestle it up upon the main deck and all Jacob could think was, "Is it enough?" The only way to find out was to have it thrown overboard and see the drag it actually produced.

Once the crew had gotten the impromptu anchor to the rear of the ship the end of the rope was securely tied off at the portside bollard, ensuring that the rope would leave the ship at a 45-degree angle to allow it to swing with the fluctuations of the current. With the anchor as secure as Jacob could make it, he had the men throw it over the side of the ship and ordered them to quickly retreat below. He was captain and would see his plan through to the end whether that end was success or failure. Max had chosen to stay with Jacob as the rope began to reel out to sea, each funnel filling quickly with water and creating ever greater directional drag, physically forcing the ship around to face into the ceaseless waves. As the funnels filled the rope's unreeling became rapid, the speed of the nylon under Jacob's guiding hand quickly rubbing the skin raw until an upraised jag of a rope caught the unprotected flesh of his hand, forcing him to recoil.

"Fuck!" he exclaimed, dropping the remaining rope to the deck as blood flowed freely from the mangled wound. "Watch that the anchor gets out safely, I've got to go staunch this," Jacob called over the wind to Max. Cupping his left hand in his right, Jacob made his way back to the safety of the hatch below, crimson tears leaking out only to dilute upon the water soaked surface of the deck. Once at the entrance to the lower deck Jacob stopped to check on Max a final time before seeking the first aid he needed. Max was a seasoned and able seaman, Jacob knew, but as he looked upon the man he could not shift the pervasive and disquieting feeling that settled over him. Peering through the sleeting salt spray, Jacob saw the rope, the rope he had dropped, jumping and twisting like a snake preparing to strike, close to where Max stood. Time seemed to slow as the cobra struck, the yellow nylon suddenly twisting around Max's left ankle, biting fast, deep and constricting about his leg in a tight knot. Before Jacob could even shout out a warning Max vanished from sight, pulled overboard as the rapidly unwinding rope jerked him from his feet without warning.

Jacob rushed to the rear of the ship, coming to a standstill in the spot where Max had just been moments before the rope pulled taught. The sudden tension sent a tandem shiver through both the Indefatigable and Jacob. Forty feet out, Jacob could see Max struggling to get free of the binding, the seaman being flung about like a ragdoll and constantly pulled below the surface by the undulating roll of the waves. Each time he surfaced, even at this distance Jacob could hear Max's desperate inhalations of life-saving air and his cries for help. At Jacob's left side stood a rack holding a fluoro orange lifesaver, its tethering line still intact; he could throw this out to Max and once Max was secured, Jacob could cut away the sea anchor's main rope, the sudden slackness in the rope giving Max the chance to free his leg and be pulled back aboard. But to cut away the sea anchor would be to condemn them all to death, even in the brief period since the rope had pulled taught the Indefatigable had started to turn to face more fully into the waves. This was the true weight of leadership, hard decisions needed to be made and some sacrifices could not be avoided. Locking eyes with Max one final time, not failing to see the terror and betrayal within the light blue orbs, Jacob made the long, slow walk back to his bunk; after all he still needed to bandage his hand.

The next few hours were perilous. The sea continued to heave and Jacob was sure that each staggering roll of the ship would be its last. The sea anchor had worked as well as could have been hoped, the Indefatigable facing the oncoming waves as head on as any rudderless ship could; she climbed falteringly up each rise to then come rushing into the trough, time and again. One would almost find the rhythmic movements hypnotic if it wasn't for the imminent death which would follow with the first failure to rise up another peak. Having retreated to his bunk after applying some basic first aid to his hand, Jacob tried to rest and he found himself now, just lying there staring up at the blank grey ceiling. Weariness had settled deep into his bones, almost aching in his need for rest though sleep continued to evade him. Each time he closed his eyes in the hopes of blissful unconsciousness naught but the accusing, baby blue stare of Max looked back at him. The guilt of what he had not done was festering in his mind, an open wound he could not leave alone. Like chapped lips you couldn't help but lick, he nagged at the memory; again and again he turned his back on those blue eyes. He could have easily saved Max, but he chose not to, he couldn't, if he had, more would have been lost by his actions. Try as he might no justification he could come up with would diminish the roiling self-blame in his head. Getting up from his bunk, joints groaning in protest at the prospect of movement, Jacob began pacing the corridors of the ship. Avoiding the crew quarters in fear of waking the remaining men he wandered absentmindedly. Monotony stilled the maelstrom that was his mind as he focused only on putting one foot in front the of the other. The simplicity of walking suffused his body as he strolled aimlessly, twisting and turning through the bowels of the ship until like a gunshot in the dark Caleb's voice stilled him.

As a dreamer startled awake Jacob was brought out of his fugue suddenly, disoriented and unsure of where he was or how he had gotten there.

Caleb ran up to him. “Sir, we’ve made it through the night, the storm is starting to abate…” There was the smallest hint of hopefulness but then his voice began to waver. “But, but we’ve lost Max…” At the mere mention of Max’s name Caleb could see Jacob go vacant, a dullness to his usual bright eyes. “Sir, Sir, Sir!” Caleb exclaimed as he shook Jacob to try and regain his attention, his previous uncertainty starting to take on a pitch of panic with the desertion of his leader’s focus.

“Yes!” Jacob unexpectedly snapped, returning to lucidity. “Max is gone. Anything more to report, Seaman?”

The hardness in his voice shocked Caleb and he wondered how Jacob could be so callous. “Well, Sir…” Caleb began tentatively, aware of the formality with which Jacob had referred to him. “We’re also missing Shane Cormac, one of the junior seaman.”

With a burst of energy clearly fuelled by anger Jacob set off down the corridor “Where could that fool have gone to?” The vehemence in his voice was unmistakable. “Rouse up the men and have them fall in on the main deck, I don’t have time for these fuckin’ idiotic games,” Jacob ordered as Caleb struggled to match his pace without running.

Gaining the main deck Jacob surveyed the assembled men. It was clear they had had just as sleepless a night as he had. Slouched and tired they littered the deck like confetti, no order, no respect. Infuriated, Jacob bellowed, “Attention! Fall in you maggots!”

Unused to such a harsh demeanour from him, all of the sailors were at first shocked but quickly fell into neat lines;

years of military service meant they knew you didn't take it lightly when a commanding officer used that tone. Clamping hands behind his back Jacob walked the lines, drawing attention to any breaches in uniform and in how some of the men had allowed their personal administration to lapse. These weren't sailors, they were slobs and he'd not tolerate it. To a man they exuded hopelessness, until Jacob walked past Ray, as neat and unperturbed as the day he had embarked the Indefatigable. Again his lips were slightly upturned, the wry smile spread across his face as if taunting Jacob to find fault with him.

"Wipe that fucking look from your damnable face and smarten up, the lot of you!" The men closest to him shied away as spittle sprayed them from his violent and unexpected outburst. "We've work to do if we are to have any hope of getting through this shit storm." Barking direct orders, Jacob split the men into groups and set them to their tasks: check the ship for any damage caused by the storm, wind in the sea anchor, get to scrounging through the ship for any food they'd missed and get the lines out to try and catch something they could eat.

All of the orders were issued with a previously unseen formality and efficiency as if Jacob expected the crew to argue with him on how the ship was being run. No complaints were issued and then men split off to do as they'd been told. Almost as an afterthought he called Ray to his side.

"Shane Cormac has gone missing, you know anything about that?" Jacob asked, the hardness in his voice showing clearly that he had already decided and was judge, jury and executioner.

"No Sir, can't say I do," Ray replied tonelessly, his lack of concern regarding a missing crewmate apparent; people would discuss the colour of their socks with more passion.

"Fall into line, were going to look for him."

Jacob walked through the Indefatigable with Ray in tow for the next two hours. With the damage to the ship caused by the initial Russian attack there were frequent dead ends and the going was slow. Finally giving up the search, Jacob dismissed Ray. Shane had either been swept overboard, had run away to hide during the storm or was simply lost within the ship. Regardless, there was nothing more anyone could do at the moment, and turning his back on a long corridor ending in a closed bulkhead, Jacob thought, "The moron will turn up somewhere."

Still more time passed as the floating hulk that was the Indefatigable drifted aimlessly on the ocean. It was two weeks since Shane and Max had… gone. In that time the remaining food stores had been completely exhausted and the crew were now restricted solely to whatever success they had at fishing. Jacob was working overtime to try and manage the fraying tempers of the men that remained, fights were now commonplace and though no weapons had been brought to bear - yet - the petty injuries were beginning to place a greater strain on the crew as a whole. They had run out of medical supplies so the petty injuries were becoming infected, and the crew further thinned as more and more became incapacitated by illness, resulting in an even heavier load on those still able to work.

As the days turned into a week malnourishment was the major issue. The heavily restricted rations that had been sustaining the crew for months had barely provided enough energy for them to complete the necessary heavy labour required to even keep the Indefatigable afloat. Now after two weeks of nothing but the occasional fish, men were starting to become bedridden and the sores inside their mouths and under their arms were developing into more serious conditions. Infection was growing at an alarming rate and with their compromised immune systems even the more healthy men were being stricken by bouts of persistent diarrhoea. Jacob thanked whoever it was that watched over him, as he had remained comparatively healthy and the malnourishment had yet to wreak havoc. The only other men that remained able bodied were Caleb, Matthew, Carlos and Ray. A darkness clouded Jacob's mind and he was unable to supress the burgeoning hatred he felt for the man. "Ray, always Ray… and that fuckin' little smile of his. Why of all the men did he have to stay healthy, stay alive?"

None of the illnesses plaguing the others seemed to be bothering Ray, no fatigue or muscle ache; other than his hawkish face appearing more sunken and ghoulish, it didn't appear as if he were affected by the lack of food at all. Consumed with frustration at the man's continued apathy, Jacob put him to work scouring the deck to remove the build-up of muck which had accompanied the few days of successful fishing they had had. Scales glittered in the sun and crunched underfoot with each step, guts were strewn about with abandon as the men had been suffused with frenzy at the mere sight of consumable flesh. All of the less palatable parts of the fish were but litter on the otherwise barren deck, and with the glare of the sun the remains were starting to rot, the stench on the ship's deck even more unpleasant than that below; a stench caused by a floor slick with the human waste from those so unwell they couldn't even make it to the latrine. Grinding a lump of fish guts into mush underfoot, Jacob watched Ray working as methodically as ever to clear away the filth. He smiled to himself. "I can think of no man more capable - no, deserving! - than Ray for such a shitty job." Feeling much better now he had made Ray's day marginally worse, Jacob retired below, making the attempt of feigned interest by checking on the infirm before taking what rest he could prior to his night watch.

Sleep was ever elusive for Jacob, with only his exhaustion causing him to lapse into unconsciousness; each time he tried to sleep there was nothing, nothing but the cold blue stare of Max's silent accusation. Even within the blissful oblivion of pure exhaustion Jacob was persecuted by nightmares of unmentionable horrors, acts harder to reconcile with than turning his back on a fellow crewmate. Yet each iteration of these horrific dreams ended with a central focus, a solitary metal door, firmly closed and promising naught but more dread should it ever be opened. There was disquiet within Jacob's mind that, while waking he could not still, however each time he took his rest the disquiet grew evermore. Jacob was unsure of what worried him most; being plagued with insomnia was terrible, it made him yearn for rest, he was becoming desperate for it and he did not know how much longer he could live like that. The thought was just laughable to him, he was far from living, and looking back on the past few months, existing was a more accurate description. Yet more worrying than his personal resilience was the realisation of the frequent sleep walking he found himself doing whenever he managed to fall into the fitful state he called sleep. Sleep walking was something which he had never been consciously aware of before. Jacob often woke from those moments of rest, if they could even be called that, in strange places within the ship, sometimes in the makeshift crew quarters, random storage rooms or up on the main deck. Each episode always ended with him having no recollection of why he was there, what he had been doing or how he had even gotten there; though each time he awoke from his midnight meander he was left with the nagging image of that locked metal door. Of course he had searched the ship, that door haunted his thoughts whether he were awake or asleep. The frequency of his searches was becoming difficult to hide from the crew, yet the irrationality of his suspicions made him hide them nonetheless. No matter how hard he searched never did he find anything, he was almost at the point where he believed the door didn't even exist but still it gnawed at the edges of his consciousness. Jacob believed the stress was getting to him, but right now he had to focus only on getting what remained of his crew home. This was the weight of leadership, a weight only he could bear and though some of the men had been lost, with others not far from succumbing to illness, he knew he had to do it, he knew he could do it, do it for them. They would survive, Jacob knew this because he knew himself to be a survivor.

Jacob was suddenly roused by Carlos, his momentary thankfulness at finding himself still in his bed quickly leaving him as he noted the frantic actions of the distressed man. Carlos' words rattled out like the staccato fire of a machinegun and at the moment just as incomprehensible to Jacob.

"Sir! Sir! They've gone! What will we do? What can we do? We needed them! Sir! Jacob! Listen to me!..." Carlos fired the questions at Jacob.

Cutting Carlos short Jacob tried to quell the panic. "Carlos! Get a hold of…"

Before he could even finish the sentence Carlos stared again. "No-no-no-no-no-no, can I make a suggestion?" Jacob did not even have time to give him the permission to keep talking. "We need to get out, Sir! Too few of us remain! We need help! We must leave…"

Jacob struck Carlos backhanded across the face to quell the torrent of statements, the retort of the slap like a sniper's bullet, silencing the relentless assault. Putting calmness into his voice while instilling it with forcefulness to command Carlos to stillness, Jacob ordered, "What happened, son? Take a breath and tell me, slowly." Jacob was concerned that he would never find out. If Carlos' heart was going as fast as his mouth surely the man would have a cardiac arrest.

Drawing a faltering breath, Carlos tried to steady himself, the words came slower and more clearly though still typically fast and with the same thick Spanish-American accent. "I found one of the other men, Sir, one of the ones who had gone missing, you know?" Each of Carlos' words continued to slow as he watched as Jacob looked askance at him.

Puzzlement clearly written on his face, Jacob asked, "So we've finally found Shane then? Where has the coward been hiding?"

Carlos now wore a look more confused than that Jacob had been just wearing. Shane had gone missing weeks ago, the whole ship had been searched, if he were alive he wasn't aboard the Indefatigable. "No, Sir…" Carlos began hesitantly, "it's Trevor… I told you he'd gone missing last week. Don't you remember?"

Self-doubt consumed Jacob, was it the insomnia? Could he really have forgotten that one of his crew had gone missing? It wasn't possible, surely this was some sort of cruel joke to test how much control he still had over the men. Masking his uncertainty with anger Jacob snapped out, "Of course I remember! Take me to him, now."

Doubt regarding his captain flickered through Carlos' eyes. "Aye, Sir, though it ain't a pretty sight, best prepare yourself."

Carlos led Jacob to the fore of the ship, right up into the cavity that made its peaked hull. Jacob could smell the rotting meat before he caught sight of the remains and didn't need to ask how Carlos had stumbled across the scene. Trevor's corpse had turned a sickly hue, a greenish yellow had replaced the healthy tan Jacob had always seen Trevor wear. Though he was in one piece and already being ravaged by decay it was clear that something far more sinister than normal decomposition had occurred; large pieces of flesh had been torn and cut away from his body. Holes had been cut into both of his cheeks, the removed flesh leaving his teeth exposed; death's grin spread across his face forevermore. Lifting up Trevor's shirt for further inspection Jacob noted the six regular holes carved into his abdomen. Trevor had been a very athletic man and had taken pride in his abs; now it appeared that someone? Something? had taken a six pack as takeaway. Jacob could not bring himself to look under the cloth that remained of his trousers; a reddish brown stain ran from mid-thigh to a thick pool, still visibly tacky on the floor at his groin.

Though the clearly deliberate dismantling of the man was horrific the amount of blood slicking the floor made it evident that Trevor had died before anything had been removed. Jacob reached down, laying his hand on Trevor's forehead and slowly, gently bringing his hand down to close the eyelids. As he paid Trevor this respect the corpse's head began to tilt forward until Jacob could see the handle of a screwdriver jutting out just below the base of Trevor's head. It was a clean blow and Jacob was only thankful that whatever monster had done this to Trevor had given him a quick death first.

Having seen all he needed to Jacob stood up, calling Carlos to his side. "You're no idiot, Carlos, you know as well as I that something seriously wrong is going on. Nonetheless we need to show Trevor the respect owed anyone who serves our country. I can't tell you who to trust for I can't believe any of my crew are capable of this… this…" Gesturing towards Trevor, his excessive hand gestures showing his dismay, Jacob could only continue numbly, "…this. Get two men you do trust, a sheet of canvas and a stretcher."

Carlos nodded his understanding and began to move off until Jacob halted him with what appeared to be an almost afterthought. "Oh, and a flag if you can find one. Once he's prepared for a sea burial I'll call the crew together" Jacob's eyes suddenly darkened, what could only be described as primordial rage stirred within their depths. "Once our respects have been paid, the hunt is on! And I know just who to start with."

Carlos confirmed his orders and rushed off to obey. Once alone Jacob dropped to his knees in front of Trevor's slumped form. Lashing out, Jacob hit the steel floor, his fist slamming into the metal with the force of all his frustration. The concussion of the blow reverberated down the hall and Jacob yelled self-accusations as his eyes welled. "How could I let this happen? How could I fail so badly as a leader to foster such insanity within the crew? Knowing I led a murderer… a monster, there must have been some way to prevent this atrocity!"

The accusations spun around in his mind for as long as it took for Jacob to register the sound of returning footsteps. Looking up Jacob saw Carlos, Caleb and Ray coming with the requested materials. Jacob couldn't believe that one of those Carlos trusted was Ray; of all the crew he could have brought with him, why Ray, that snake? Swallowing the bile he suddenly tasted simply upon viewing the man and with a great deal of effort resisting the urge to lash out at him for his typical sardonic smile - Sick fuck! Was he so twisted as to think this funny? - Jacob put the men to work quickly. Trevor was placed upon the stretcher, wrapped in canvas to give him some amount of privacy and then a tattered American flag was draped over his prone form. Carlos confessed to taking the flag from the pole on the main deck as it was all he could find.

Leading the procession to the main deck Jacob called all men to attendance, those sickly or injured not excused from paying their respects. Service was a personal debt required by their country and Jacob ensured all knew the true cost. Once all the men had assembled Jacob was appalled, not with them but with himself; it was not just Trevor, Max and Shane missing, the crew was now whittled down to six in total. All that remained were two of the ship's cooks, Carlos, Caleb, Ray and Jacob himself. Jacob could not believe how the crew had gotten so small in just the last few weeks. How was he not aware of so many missing men? Though, more importantly, where had they gone? A cold sweat began to bead his forehead at the thought of more men meeting the same fate as Trevor.

Jacob proceeded to give Trevor a proper sea burial, espousing the qualities of the man, commending his service to state and country, finally acknowledging the hole that would be left with his passing. For all the generic pleasantries he said, Jacob's mind was solely focused upon the five men standing before him; it was a limited pool of choices to choose a killer from and Jacob now cursed himself for maintaining the rigid discipline. The men had adopted an air of typical military dispassion, their respect serving to do nothing but mask any nervousness from the proceeding. As the eulogy drew to a close Jacob called Carlos forward to join him, both men taking a hold of one of the wooden poles that made up the stretcher. With the coarse timber in hand they slowly raised the end of the stretcher until Trevor's remains began to slide down the canvas, the flag rippling as his body passed beneath until finally a nondescript package fell into the sea. Once completed Jacob returned his attention to the men assembled in front of him; the distrust between them had already set in and was clearly seen in how much distance they kept between themselves. Word must have already spread among them about Trevor's demise. Any one of them could be the killer and Jacob was going to find out who it was, but for now he wanted to let the mistrust fester. Constant vigilance would make them all safer as individuals and sooner or later the killer would be revealed. With a final measuring glance Jacob dismissed them.

Life aboard the Indefatigable continued and Jacob persevered despite his fitful sleep. The stress of leadership was made unmanageable by having the killer aboard, and this stress caused more than just Jacob to sleep with one eye open lest they be the next to go missing. The problem with insomnia is you're never truly awake, things happen as if muted; full conversations occurred as nothing more than exaggerated miming and the oddly snatched word here or there. Each time Jacob did manage to get any semblance of rest it was short lived and now his dreams showed nothing but that locked steel door, a door which now seemed to glow red around the edges and was as ever elusive during his renewed daytime searches. It had not taken long, three maybe four days, Jacob did not really know anymore, the days had begun to blend together, and then Caleb was gone.

With another member going missing the remainder of the crew fractured, a catastrophic breakdown of any remaining bonds of trust. Each man took up whatever weapons they could find in addition to their own service issued side arms and dispersed throughout the ship. Each man was intent on building his own personal sanctuary, ensuring his own safety and survival. The rules of the game had changed, no longer was this an investigation, or an inquisition, it was survival at the most primeval level. Each sailor was no longer concerned with the outcome for their fellow men, this was about themselves and their safety, and no longer would there be any hesitation in protecting themselves. By using any means necessary they ensured they would see another day even if those that they had called crewmates did not. As with the others Jacob had set up his own sanctuary; his space was a single entry room in the mid ship, one way in and one way out. Though he watched the door like a hawk, waiting for the slightest move to swoop upon his prey he had a sense of security, almost peace. His existence had changed from a life of leadership and stress to one of solitary stoicism, and he felt the weight lift from his shoulders knowing he had only himself to look after.

Another two days passed with the crew similarly dispersed throughout the ship, however as time dragged on Jacob could hear someone moving around. Whether they were looking for a fresh kill or to scavenge food Jacob did not know; and looking back on what had fractured the crew so dramatically he was not really sure there was a difference anymore. Footsteps that seemed deliberately light approached his sanctuary. Taking cover in the corner of the room behind a barrier erected of dismantled storage shelves Jacob trained his Glock at the single point of entry. The handle to the door moved, hesitantly at first but slowly it crept down, creaking as the metal slide securing the door scraped back into its sleeve. A trickle of cold sweat crept down his neck and the movement of the handle was mirrored by Jacob, his finger tightening incrementally on his side arm's trigger. As Jacob prepared for the first burst of fire the latch stopped moving and then returned just as slowly to its locked position. Jacob did not loosen the grip on his weapon or the pressure he applied to the trigger. He waited, not hearing any retreating steps, not being foolish enough to fall into such a poorly disguised trap he set himself for this perceived Mexican standoff. After what seemed an eternity the first footfall sounded down the hall, followed quickly by another receding into the distance.

Unable to curb his curiosity Jacob opened the door in time to see Ray's retreating from rounding the corner at the end of the corridor. As they always say though, it's curiosity that killed the cat. Walking forward Jacob did not notice the rudimentary trip wire set up at his door's entrance. Breaking the line released the tension on the broken spar of a bent over stretcher post. Taken by surprise by the trap Jacob could not suppress the "Ah! Fuck!" as the jagged end of the pole ripped into the top of his right thigh; biting deeply, the ragged wound caused his blood to flow and the pain intensified as the leg bore his weight. Knowing he would be the next victim if he did not move quickly, for the trap was designed to pin him in place and waste time allowing for the stalker to sneak up on him, Jacob swiftly pulled the makeshift spear from his leg, his haste only further damaging the already torn flesh. Applying pressure, Jacob tried to staunch the leaking wound and tearing strips away from his shirt quickly wrapped the leg. The dirty cloth quickly stained crimson as his blood saturated the basic dressing.

Testing his weight on the wounded leg sent waves of fire coursing through his thigh. He knew he could still move but was not naïve enough to think that he could move swiftly or with anything that resembled stealth. Taking his first faltering steps Jacob began to give chase. Venomously he spat under his breath, "I'll take the offence straight to Ray. That piece of shit! I'll not wait, cowering like a whipped dog waiting for death." Limping down the corridor Jacob followed an unruly path, the broken shuffle and uneven gait lending its own horrific and ghoulish air to Jacob's silhouette. The turns seemed to come at random, though he felt as if he were compelled down this route; left, right, right, left, the turns continued to come and disoriented Jacob until he finally found himself at the inevitable dead end. Here he stood in front of a cold, locked door; a door familiar, the stuff of nightmares already beginning to fray the edges of his resolution.

A blinding flash of white light, in complete contrast to the darkness which had consumed his life for the past months, startled him awake. The sudden wakefulness was confusing as it was composed of an assault of strange sensations. Jacob was amazed to find himself in bed, he did not even remember going to bed at all; nor did he know how he had gotten into what appeared to be a hospital. His bed was made of coarse white linen, odd-coloured stains dotted the blanket here and there and drew his attention to the usual mixture of smells; the bleach, shit and piss which perfumed the space of every hospital he had ever stayed in. Looking around, he noticed the walls were split in half, the bottom painted a sickly pastel green and the top pure white. A shocking wood balustrade ran around the entire room where the colours met. It had to be a larger room as a peach-coloured curtain had been drawn, blocking any view of the other patients though admitting the endless sounds of their misery and the monotonous tones of their monitoring equipment. The room was lit from a single small window on the eastern wall, the bars on that window throwing pinstriped shadows across the bed he lay in. Jacob's focus began to wane and he found himself watching the shadowy cage drifting across the bed with the movements of the sun. After an immeasurable amount of time Jacob came back to lucidity, only now noticing the raised white plastic rails on his bed, securing him from rolling out and adding physical reinforcement to his ethereal prison. With this moment of clarity came memories, horrific memories, and memories of the ordeal aboard the Indefatigable. The months came back and culminated in a single night; running for his life and falling, his prone form vulnerable as the shadowy figure whom he assumed to be Ray descending upon him. He wondered, with equal measures of confusion and relief that he was still alive, "How did I get here? Have I been saved or is this what comes after death?" Sitting up fully he was immediately overcome with nausea, "At least I didn't imagine the head wound," he thought sarcastically as the dizziness passed. Lying back down to make his head stop spinning, Jacob made to reach over and probe at the wound with his right hand. That thought abruptly ended as his hand was caught fast against a relentless, biting cold. Propping himself up on an elbow Jacob saw that he was handcuffed to those guard rails. Knowing they were to keep him for escaping rather than prevent him from rolling out of bed had his anxiety spiking.

A cold sweat began to prickle his skin. The curtain to his left was reefed aside, its plastic rings clattering along the old metal rod. Moving to stand at the foot of his bed three men entered the room. All three were dressed impeccably in the uniform of military officials. Clad in stiffly pressed black suits, their highly polished brass buttons glinted in the meagre sunlight. Multi-coloured stripes adorned their breast pockets, denoting the actions they had served in. From the strips of red, black and white as well as the lines of black, white, green and magenta, Jacob could tell these men had all seen action across Afghanistan and Iraq. It was the man in the middle with the longest line of distinguishing colours that worried Jacob the most; blues and magenta, yellow, green and red. This man had seen action in not only Afghanistan and Iraq but had been active in Kosovo and Vietnam. When a warrior such as this man looked at you with such a stern set to his face you would be foolish to not be concerned. Jacob surveyed the three men as a unit; the men to the left and right were expressionless, their eyes displayed no hint of empathy or compassion. Jacob supposed that would be part of the job after seeing the bold white MP printed on their armbands. Jacob noticed how quickly his anxiety changed; there is an understandable panic that comes over any serviceman when they are handcuffed to a bed under the supervision of two military police.

Jacob did his best, and failed, to stifle the panic and paid much closer attention to the man in the centre. After reviewing the service he had given to his country he looked surprising spry for his age, he would have been in his mid-sixties at the latest, with a clean shaven face the only real sign of his years being the thick salt and pepper hair that topped his head; his baby blue eyes, so similar to Max's, held both warmth and a razor sharp edge. When he brought his arms from behind his back Jacob could see the three wide golden bands at the end of each sleeve; this man was a captain and Jacob hastily and clumsily tried to form the semblance of a salute

Waving aside Jacob's panicked movements he began, his voice deep and sonorous, "Jacob Rosswell, I am Anthony Carter, Captain of USS Vengeance. Firstly I must let you know that the war has ended…"

Jacob's initial rush of elation at surviving the war was quickly tempered by his current situation.

The Captain continued as if not noticing the torrent of emotions cross Jacob's face, "Secondly I have been called upon to lead the group of your peers casting sentence at your court martial." All warmth had left the captain's eyes and Jacob went just as cold. What was he talking about? He had done nothing but try to survive the hell that is war!

The captain continued despite the obvious anger showing on Jacob's face. "You are accused of the murder of fellow crewmates Caleb Hortega and Trevor Simpson. Furthermore you are charged with the manslaughter of Max Hughes." The captain's eyes were honed to a killing edge with each added accusation, an end to which never seemed to come. "… and lastly, due to the neglect of duties inherent in your post as acting captain you are suspected of professional misconduct resulting in the deaths of more than ten men…"

Before Captain Carter could finish the full list of accusations Jacob burst out, anger and shock adding conviction to his words, "It wasn't me! I didn't do anything but try to have my crew survive as best as I could." Jacob's eyes flickered to the faces of each of the men arrayed in front of him, desperation clearly growing with each statement,."If you want to find the real killer, I'll lead you to him, it was Ray. I know it was him!"

A flash of pity surged through the captain's eyes, "Jacob!" he snapped, trying to gain the hysterical man's attention. Keeping his tone formal and slowing his speech to make each word clear, he continued, "This is the third time we have had this conversation. This is my last attempt at speaking with you to get you to remember what happened and understand what is going on here."

Though the words were clear they still made no sense to Jacob.

"Your court martial is drawing to a close and we're expecting a unanimous decision. For the final time there never was, nor has there ever been a Ray serving aboard the Indefatigable." He could see Jacob's disbelief written on his face before the protests even began.

“There had to be! I saw him, he was the one who wounded my leg…”

The captain cut Jacob short, frustration at his repeated conversation adding anger to his, until now unperturbed voice, “Jacob, there is NO wound to your leg. Furthermore in that… room…” Carter had seen some unmentionable events in his life, but nothing he had ever seen in any theatre of war would haunt him as much as that room did. Taking a deep breath to slow his pulse, he carried on as per his duty. “In the room there was only one set of fingerprints and the significant amount of forensic evidence is all linked to you.” The captain watched as Jacob's eyes began to glaze

Jacob’s attention was caught by a movement to Carter’s left, that peach curtain began to rustle as if caught in a breeze yet the only window in the room had remained shut. Then Ray came into view, silently as if materialising out of the shadows of the curtain. Ray locked eyes with Jacob just as Jacob himself began issuing warnings to the captain.

“Ray’s behind you! Watch out Sir!”

Jacob began to calm, seeing no reaction from any of the assembled men. Then for the first time Jacob had ever noticed, Ray’s characteristic smirk changed, his face contorted with a madman’s merriment as high pitched, manic laughter issued from a frame too small to make such discordant sound.

Taking another deep breath, Captain Carter turned his back to Jacob, frustrated… he’d heard these ravings before. Storming out of the room he passed straight through Ray, his spectre dispersing as a windblown fog. A final contemptuous glare from the captain was the last Jacob remembered as the peach curtain was yanked across, drawing his life to a close.

www.ingramcontent.com/pod-product-compliance
Lightning Source LLC
Chambersburg PA
CBHW020941310726
48980CB00001B/8

* 9 7 8 0 6 4 8 1 0 3 0 8 0 *